SPECIAL MESSAGE TO READERS

NIGHT CREATURES

After the worst storm in memory, strange things started happening in Frankport, Michigan. A teenage boy was murdered in full view of his friends. Reed Devlin spent the night with a ghost — a woman who'd already been reported dead that evening. And Reed's old army buddy was killed by two weird, half-seen *things*. Something evil had come to Frankport. But for what purpose? And how would Frankport protect itself against a demon that was over ten thousand years old?

STEVE HAYES AND
DAVID WHITEHEAD

NIGHT
CREATURES

Complete and Unabridged

LINFORD
Leicester

First published in Great Britain

First Linford Edition
published 2013

British Library CIP Data

Hayes, Steve.
   Night creatures. - - (Linford mystery library)
   1. Suspense fiction.
   2. Large type books.
   I. Title II. Series III. Whitehead, David,
   1958 –
   813.5′4–dc23

   ISBN 978–1–4448–1437–8

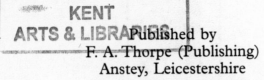

Published by
F. A. Thorpe (Publishing)
Anstey, Leicestershire

Set by Words & Graphics Ltd.
Anstey, Leicestershire
Printed and bound in Great Britain by
T. J. International Ltd., Padstow, Cornwall

This book is printed on acid-free paper

1

It was a hell of a night . . . and a night for hell. Gale-driven rain lashed at the small, once-prosperous town of Frankport, Michigan. It stitched across pot-holed streets where nobody lived anymore and formed large, bubbling puddles where poorly-maintained drains could no longer cope with the volume. Overhead, thunder cracked and rumbled almost without pause and vast, flickering sheets of lightning flared at regular intervals to reveal a sky contused by low, scudding clouds.

On Main Street each successive flash revealed just how many stores had gone out of business in the past twelve months. Their number was shocking. The closure of the Chrysler and GM Auto plants had signaled a death-knell for the town. The Express Airways freight line had followed shortly afterward and that had been the *coup de grâce*, the blow that finally killed stone-dead any hope of recovery.

Now all that seemed to thrive in Frankport were signs that said *BANK OWNED* or *FORECLOSURE*. They, it seemed, multiplied by the day.

There was another discharge of lightning, and the rain started falling even harder.

It may have been nothing more than imagination — this was, after all, easily the worst storm anyone in Frankport could remember — but the chilly air seemed to carry with it an air of . . . not so much *expectancy* as . . . *apprehension*.

Wait for it . . .

Wait for it . . .

And then there came another prolonged crash of thunder, the kind that makes the ground shiver underfoot . . . and this one made it sound as if someone had just breached the gates of Hell.

Which, as it later turned out, they had.

★ ★ ★

Just outside of town, a sorry-looking scarecrow stood in the middle of a field full of withered, rain-sodden corn shoots.

Dressed in an old check jacket, a cast-off turtleneck sweater and worn-thin jeans, it had a straw-stuffed body and an old, floppy-brimmed homburg affixed atop his head. The head was just a straw-filled bag tied crudely at the neck. But someone had done their best to add an illusion of reality by sewing bright blue buttons close together for its eyes, a small triangle of some darker material to simulate a nose and a length of red ribbon that was meant to signify a smile but instead looked like a grimace.

A wooden frame had been threaded through its clothes prior to stuffing, so that now it leaned at a slight angle, with its arms outstretched like a life-size rag-doll Jesus. Rain dribbled down its canvas face like tears.

Without warning, a bolt of lightning struck the scarecrow. Instantly it was charred black. What was left fell loosely into the mud.

It was then that a very curious thing happened.

Something dark and sluggish began to

trickle from between the scarecrow's outstretched corn fingers.

Blood.

Human blood.

The blood found a rut in the swampy ground and immediately began to follow its course, gradually diluting until it became a near translucent pink.

On it ran until eventually it reached a peculiar mark in the mud between the cornrows. The mark was a four-inch oval with a distinctive V-split at its top end, the split extending for about a third of its overall length. Here the blood continued to fill the shape until it overflowed and then ran on to a similar track about two feet away.

If anyone had been around to see them they would have quickly identified them as cloven hoof-prints, for they continued on for some distance at regular two-foot intervals, one right hoof, one left.

But what kind of hoofed animal only walked on two legs?

The tracks continued on through the mud until they gradually grew less defined and appeared to somehow spread

4

and lengthen until . . .

. . . until . . .

Until they resembled the prints of bare human feet.

The feet of a human female.

The stride somewhat longer now, the tracks led on through the mire and out onto the two-lane highway that ran parallel to the field.

Whoever — whatever — had made them was heading for town.

And judging by the soft, assorted rustles and crackles that still came from the cornfield, the half-heard sounds of eager breathing and assorted giggles, the flash of moonlight on violet eyes or saliva-wet teeth, he, she or it was not alone.

About a mile back, a Mack semi hauling a forty-foot refrigerated trailer filled with poultry meal barreled along the blacktop. Rain lashed against the fogged windshield, coming so hard now that even the constant metronomic sweep of the wipers could hardly keep the view ahead from distorting almost beyond recognition.

Hunched forward over the wheel, as if that might help him see clearer, Ned Cross shook his head at the appalling conditions and just kept going. A quick glance at the speedometer told him he was pushing eighty; way above the limit for a truck this size and way more than the mitten state's night-time limit allowed; but that was just too bad. In this job you were always hurrying to make up for lost time.

Ned was about thirty or so, with curly fair hair cut into a mullet and a flabby fifty-inch waist. That was another thing about this job, he thought; you spent too much time sitting behind the wheel eating junk food.

On the seat beside him the scattered remains of his supper stabbed him with guilt — crunchy red-corn tortillas filled with ground beef and hot sauce, a bowl of pinto beans swimming in three kinds of cheese, a bag of cinnamon twists, tortilla chips covered in beans and jalapenos and soft-flour wraps stuffed with seasoned rice and yet more double-portions of ground beef, all courtesy of Taco Bell.

But then he grinned suddenly. Hell, maybe it wasn't guilt after all. Maybe it was just heartburn he was experiencing.

He was half-listening to the sport jocks chattering away on WDUN when he saw her, and by then it was way too late.

She was standing in the center of the highway with her back to him, wearing a black vinyl raincoat with the hood up. His headlights threw her shadow out ahead of her and their reflections sparkled and skittered along the folds in her raincoat like falling stars. He saw she was carrying some kind of bag or slim case over one shoulder —

Then he thought: *Shit!*

He hit the brakes and twisted the wheel in an effort to avoid her.

Tires wailing, the truck immediately skidded out of control, the trailer behind it slewing drunkenly from left to right like the wagging of a lazy dog's tail. The sleeper cab lurched, slid on, the asphalt grinding rubber off the treads, and then somehow it managed to right itself before juddering to a halt halfway across the shoulder.

Badly shaken, Ned felt his dinner threaten to make a return appearance and hurriedly sucked air to keep it down. With pounding heart he automatically switched on his hazards, grabbed his flashlight and half-fell out of the cab into the storm.

Rain and wind hammered him as he stumbled to the front of the truck. He braced himself for the sight he expected to see; the remains of the girl splattered all over his radiator.

But the grille was clean except for a few spattered bugs.

Surprised, he bent down and shone the light under the truck.

He could see nothing there.

Straightening up, he shivered. His shirt was already plastered to his body, his hair sticking to his forehead and neck like fresh-dug worms. Belly bouncing, he splashed through the rain to the rear of the trailer, made a quick search and once again came up empty.

Frowning, he played the light back along the rainy highway and then along both grassy shoulders. There was no sign of the girl anywhere.

Where the hell *was* she? He knew he hadn't imagined her.

He tried to remember the sound she'd made hitting the radiator and couldn't. And yet he knew with bleak certainty that he couldn't have missed her. There hadn't been time for that.

A foot of water ran in a fast torrent along a ditch beside the road. He went closer, the flashing hazard lights playing an amber-tinted *now-you-see-me, now-you-don't* game with his hunched shadow. Cautiously he peered into the ditch but saw noth —

He suddenly heard a new sound above the roar of the storm — a piercing kind of *trill* — and a moment later a large brown screech owl swooped down at him as if out of nowhere.

Startled, he cried out and instinctively dropped the flashlight in order to swat it away. Refusing to be intimidated, the bird fluttered noisily around his head, trilling all the while, its talons shredding his left cheek and drawing blood.

Ned stumbled backward, had a fleeting glimpse of its eyes — vivid yellow, the pupils small and round and, given the creature's otherwise frantic animation, somehow curiously *dead* — and then it slashed at him again and he screwed his own eyes shut and swung a desperate punch at it.

His knuckles only connected with air, and when he opened his eyes again the screech owl was nowhere to be seen.

He looked around, eyelids flickering in the rain.

The bastard was gone. But his face was stinging, and when he touched it with the tips of his fingers they came away red with blood.

' . . . *sonofabitch* . . . '

Warily he went after the flashlight and snatched it up with a sudden surge of anger. Then he walked back alongside the truck, wrenched open the door and hauled himself up inside.

The WDUN sports jocks were still babbling inanely as he slammed the door behind him.

He sat there for a moment, dripping blood and rainwater. Then he dug out his first aid kit and hastily cleaned and

10

patched the scratches. They weren't deep and wouldn't need stitching; wouldn't even leave scars. But he told himself he'd better get a tetanus shot in the morning.

When he was finished he stared through the windshield, trying to figure out what had become of the girl and already starting to wonder if she'd even been there to begin with. And yet —

He was just about to get out of the cab and make one more search when something fast and dark scurried through the beams of his headlights — actually a whole *pack* of somethings — and then vanished into the darkness on the other side of the highway.

Instinctively he reared back. What the fuck *were* they? His first thought was rats, but they were too big for that; in fact, they varied in size. Feral swine, then? Could be. Then again, the way the rain was even now battering the windshield and warping his view of the highway beyond, they could have been just about anything.

Still . . .

He decided against making another

search for the girl.

Instead he gunned the engine and drove off, still wondering what the fuck had happened to her. He decided he'd better report this in Frankport, if only to cover his ass. And that meant he'd now have even more time to make up, dammit.

* * *

Rainwater continued to race along the ditch beside the road. It was deeper now and moving even faster. Suddenly a woman's leg, wearing a red stiletto-heeled pump, thrust to the surface. For a few moments the leg thrashed wildly as if its owner were trying to reach the surface, but the fast-moving current held her down. Then the thrashing slowed and finally stopped and the leg sank below the water again.

* * *

A half-mile further on, Ned Cross's headlights picked out a sign that said

12

WELCOME TO FRANKPORT. As his truck passed it by, the sign collapsed and was swept away by the churning red water.

2

Down at the High School football stadium, the storm had turned the field into a shallow, muddy lake. Rain battered the rows of tiered metal benches, creating a racket that almost drowned the booming thunder above.

But Reed Devlin hardly noticed it.

Dressed in old and now-soaked desert camouflage fatigues, Reed sat as still as a fencepost directly below the metal scoreboard, seemingly oblivious to the danger it presented in such wild conditions.

But then, Reed and danger were old friends. A retired US Marine Corps major, he'd fought practically a hundred hours straight during the liberation of Kuwait; had engaged enemy mortar positions with nothing more than a .50-calibre Barrett sniper rifle; supported tank companies in the cramped, insurgent-filled streets of Fallujah. He'd provided reconnaissance under fire; spotted for an 81mm artillery team and engaged in fighting so heavy during his tour in Afghanistan that it had claimed the lives of twenty of his men and sent another thirty home as amputees.

After that, this didn't even rate as a stroll in the park.

Reed was in his early forties, with short, rain-darkened sandy-blond hair and pale brows above well-spaced blue eyes. He had a straight nose with flared nostrils and a wide mouth above a pointed jaw that was crying out to be shaved. He still carried a hundred-ninety pounds on his six-one frame, and under other circumstances could have easily personified the perfect, all-American hero.

But these were not other circumstances. This was the here and now, and the truth was that Reed was closer to being an alcoholic than a hero.

Deciding to drink to that, he raised an almost-empty bottle of Seagram's VO to his lips and drained it dry.

Just then a streak of lightning struck the scoreboard. There was a vicious *crack*, a firework cascade of falling sparks accompanied by a harsh *fzzttt* of sound . . . and then the scoreboard fragmented. Debris crashed down around Reed and bounced and rolled off the metal benches before coming to rest in the soggy field below.

Still Reed hardly seemed to notice. His only reaction was to slowly turn his face toward the angry sky and let the rain pebble his skin as he thought: *Can't You do better than that? I'm right here, damn You! Now take aim and try it again!*

But even drunk as he was, he knew better than to expect a response. He'd spent his whole life waiting for God to finish him off and it hadn't happened yet — and frankly he was getting real tired of waiting. *Real* tired . . .

I ought to go home, he thought blearily.

Even as he thought it, something brushed against the backs of his legs and then was gone. Startled, Reed lurched up out of his seat and thought: . . . *the fuck was that?*

He saw them then, or as much as the pouring rain would allow him to see: dark, darting shapes chasing each other

16

all the way across benches and off into the shadows at the edge of the field. *Rats*, he thought, and pulled a face.

And yet they'd been pretty large for rats, hadn't they?

He shook his head. That was all Frankport needed on top of everything else — an infestation of giant mutated rats.

His sodden fatigues stuck to him, chilling him to the bone. Swaying, he hurled the empty bottle into the night; then, favoring his left leg, he limped unsteadily from the stadium.

Outside, he paused briefly to watch a bedraggled rag-doll with red shoes, that had gotten wedged in the mouth of a drain that was already choking on excess rainwater. Swept toward the waste pipe by the strong current, the doll's arms and legs flailed as if it were trying to save itself, until at last it vanished from sight.

An obnoxious *whoop* of sound — a siren — made him turn around and squint straight into the revolving red and blue lights of a Frankport PD patrol car.

'Hey, Major, wanna ride?'

The cop who'd yelled the offer was Jack Kelsey, a short, olive-skinned man of about thirty, with a jowly face and a permanent five o'clock shadow. Reed eyed him cynically for a moment before saying: 'Only if you're going to hell.'

Kelsey gave him a weird look, and shrugged. 'I'll take that as a no.'

He pulled his head back into the car and drove away. Reed watched him go. Once upon a time Kelsey might have tried to talk him around. *Come on now, Major, you don't really want to catch pneumonia, do you?*

But not anymore. The town was getting as sick and tired of Reed as Reed was getting of himself.

Which made it unanimous.

The sooner he was dead and buried, the better it would be for everyone.

* * *

Seemingly oblivious to the storm, the screech owl that had attacked Ned Cross perched on the spire of St Mark's church on Chaffee Street. From here it could see the entire town — or what was left of it after being hit by the recession.

It was a small municipality much like any other, albeit a little more run-down than most. There was a county court-house and a hospital, a park with a lake and a bandstand and a train station that had optimistically been turned into suites of offices after the trains stopped running back in '03. But at street-level things were very different. Weeds were starting to sprout on the sidewalks. Garbage was now only collected every second week in order to save money, causing the air to stink. At eleven thirty every night the streetlights that used to glow from dusk till dawn were switched off, plunging the town into darkness. The main library had closed down a week earlier; for good, they said.

And there were other things, too, things you couldn't see but couldn't help but sense. Tension. Despair. Desperation. And perhaps strongest of all, anger — the feeling that everyone was on a short fuse; that even the silliest thing could make your best friend go grab a gun and shoot you dead.

Frankport, Michigan.
Population . . . dwindling.

⋆　⋆　⋆

In his comfortable, cluttered office at the back of the church Father Paul Benedict was on the phone with Bishop Teal who — not to put too fine a point on it — was giving him holy hell.

'It boils down to this,' said the bishop, his voice cold and mechanical, much like the man himself. 'Unless you find a way to build up your congregation, you'll be asked to retire. Do I make myself clear?'

Father Benedict closed his hazel eyes and nodded wearily. They'd been through this before, many times, although Bishop Teal had always stopped short of giving such an ultimatum.

'I *said*, do I make myself clear?'

'Yes, Your Excellency,' Benedict replied patiently. 'But if I could just make *you* understand how grim the employment situation is here, and how the population has shrunk — '

'I'm well aware of that, Paul.'

'Then you're equally well aware that I have an uphill struggle on my hands. These people, those who've stayed on because there's simply nowhere else for them to go, they feel as if they've been *abandoned*, Your Excellency. And frankly, I can't say I blame them.'

'What happened there, what's happened all across the *country*, is regrettable,' said Bishop Teal. 'But it was the fault of the government, Paul, the government and the banks — not of the church.'

'Of course. But when these people turn to the church for answers, to try to make sense out of why so many of them gave their entire working lives to the very companies who then laid them off, when they need to be reassured that everything will be okay . . . frankly, Your Excellency, I don't know what to tell them. They feel the church has let them down, and so do I.'

There was a long moment of silence at the other end of the line. Then Bishop Teal said: 'I think perhaps I should pretend I didn't hear that.'

But having started, Father Benedict

refused to quit. 'Maybe that's the problem,' he persisted. 'Maybe we've closed our eyes and our ears and perhaps even our hearts for too long. Maybe that's why my congregation is shrinking — because they don't believe we're interested in what becomes of them, only how heavy the collection plate is.'

Bishop Teal drew a shocked breath. 'How *dare* you say that!' he hissed.

'I'm not saying that's the way it *is*, Your Excellency — only that that's the way my congregation *perceive* it to be.'

'Then make them perceive things more accurately,' snapped the bishop. 'The church *does* care for them. Of *course* it does. But we have problems too, Paul. This recession has hit everyone, and just like Chrysler and General Motors, we have to downsize if we're to survive.'

'Downsize!' Father Benedict couldn't help but snort. 'That's a word these people have come to despise. It's a word *I* despise. It dehumanizes us, Your Excellency, it somehow detaches the decisions we make from their consequences. It's a word that businessmen use, not bishops.'

'*Matthew seven-one*,' warned the bishop.

Father Benedict smiled sourly. *Judge not lest ye be judged*.

'Maybe there's another reason you're losing your congregation, Paul,' continued Bishop Teal. 'Maybe they don't want an old man lecturing them anymore. Maybe it's time for new blood.'

For one reckless moment Father Benedict felt like playing the bishop at his own game. *Timothy five-one-two*, he'd say, and Bishop Teal, remembering his bible, would think: *Do not rebuke an older man but encourage him as you would a father*.

Instead he heard himself say: 'Are you threatening me, by any chance, Your Excellency?'

'I won't even dignify that with a reply.'

'No, of course not. I'm sorry. But when you use that tone with me, I feel the way my congregation must have felt when they were 'downsized'. And it's a bitter pill to swallow. It makes them question the bigger plan.'

'I'm not interested in excuses, Paul, just results. *Get* them.'

The line went dead.

Father Benedict replaced the receiver with exquisite care and drew a long, pensive breath. After a moment he looked up at the crucifix on the wall facing him. 'You're lucky,' he told it. 'In your day you didn't have to deal with recessions.'

Father Benedict stood up and winced at the pain in the small of his back. Perhaps the bishop was right. Perhaps he, Benedict, should make way for new blood.

He caught sight of himself in the old beveled mirror that hung from the back of the closed, arched door. The reflection showed him a compact seventy year-old of average height, with neatly-trimmed white hair parted to the left and a clipped chevron moustache that was just a shade darker. He had a pleasant enough face that was now rounded out by age, and strangely — given his calling — undeniably Mephistophelian eyebrows above pale blue eyes.

He looked back at himself and thought: *Well, there it is. After months of beating around the bush, Bishop Teal has finally set his cards on the table. Unless you find a way to build up your congregation, you'll be forced to retire.*

But was that such a bad thing?

Father Benedict didn't even have to think about it. Of course it was. For one thing, the church was all he had, all he'd ever had. Take that away from him and he had nothing at all. For another, he had always intended to die in harness, spreading the word of the Lord and bringing succor to the needy right unto his final breath.

Troubled, he decided to seek solace in prayer and went quietly through to the church. Empty at this hour — a little after eight-thirty in the evening — it was lit softly and comfortingly peaceful. He went directly to the altar and knelt before the life-size Christ on the cross, where he closed his eyes and clasped his hands.

Lord Jesus, may everything I do begin with You, continue with Your help, and be done under Your guidance. May my sharing in the Mass free me from my sins, and make me worthy of Your healing. May I grow in Your Love and —

Behind him he heard a soft sound, perhaps a cough.

He turned, peered into the shadows that had gathered around the stoup at the far end of the church and saw nothing.

As he faced the altar again he heard the sound once more. It was a soft clearing of the throat.

Curious now, he rose and walked quietly up the aisle, carefully checking each pew as he went, glancing once at the confessional to make sure it was empty.

A girl was stretched out on the very last pew, her head, with its thick spill of long, wavy strawberry-blonde hair, resting on a computer bag.

He looked down at her. She was in her twenties, certainly no older. She wore a black vinyl raincoat and was barefoot. Her shoes, red stiletto-heeled pumps that seemed out of place in a rainstorm, lay under the pew, where she had kicked them off. Next to them was a pile of lipstick-tipped cigarette butts.

Sight of the butts angered Father Benedict. This show of disrespect capped what had been a truly miserable day. He

26

barked: 'You! Young woman! Wake up!'

His voice echoed around the church.

When the girl didn't move, he was tempted to give her an angry shake. 'Young woman!' he said again.

At last she stirred and sat up sleepily. Her hair was so long it fell to the small of her back.

'Huh? What . . . ?'

Her voice was deep, husky, almost obscenely sensual.

'This is a house of God,' he told her stiffly. 'Not a flophouse. And *certainly* not an ashtray.'

She stretched. 'Okay. Don't give yourself a wedgy.'

She had an oval-shaped face and clear, pale skin. Her brow was fine, her nose small, her lips heart-shaped, her jaw well-defined. She yawned and wearily rubbed her curiously violet eyes. Digging into her pockets, she came up with a crumpled cigarette pack. A quick peek showed her that it was empty.

'Don't suppose you got a smoke on you?'

Father Benedict drew himself up to his

full height. 'I want you to leave,' he said firmly. 'Right now.'

'You gotta be kidding! It's pissing buckets out there!'

'I said *leave*.'

'What happened to 'Give me your tired, your poor, your huddled masses'?'

'That's the Statue of Liberty,' he said, 'not the Catholic Church. Now, get out!'

She stared at him for a long time, as if expecting him to have a change of heart. When he didn't, she hissed: 'You'll *pay* for this.'

Grudgingly she stuffed her feet into her discarded shoes, then picked up the computer bag and stormed off toward the door. 'Some man of God *you* are!' she called back disdainfully.

A moment later she slammed the door behind her.

3

The lock was loose and the door didn't close completely. As it flew back on its hinges wind-whipped rain blew inside, drenching everything. Muttering irritably, Father Benedict hurried over and, after a considerable struggle, managed to close the door.

He turned around and leaned against the oak panels, breathing hard. The woman's words echoed in his ears.

Some man of God you are!

She's right, he thought sadly. After all, how could he have turned *anyone* out on a night like this?

Troubled by his conscience, he offered up a simple prayer even as he opened the door again and trotted out after her. *Lord Jesus, I am sorry for my sins, I renounce Satan and all his works, And I give you my life —*

He stopped on the steps and looked in both directions.

There was no sign of her on the dark, storm-lashed street.

His head dropped and his shoulders slumped and all at once he felt incredibly, completely bone-weary. *Forgive me, Lord, for letting my personal problems cloud my judgment —*

'Having a bad day, Father?'

He looked up, rain dripping from his eyelashes and the tip of his nose, just as Reed Devlin came limping out of the darkness toward him. Surprised, he descended the steps to meet him. Reed's limp, Father Benedict knew, was a legacy of his tour of duty in Afghanistan. But it was whisky that made him seem more unsteady than usual.

'I've had better,' Father Benedict replied when he was close enough.

Reed stopped in the open gateway at the far end of the stone path. Buffeted by the wind he stood there, grinning. 'No shit.'

Father Benedict ignored the profanity. 'What're you doing out on a godforsaken night like this?'

'Checking on the flight patterns of the Canada Goose.'

'Haven't lost your sense of humor, I see.'

'Where would I be *without* it?'

Father Benedict studied him through the downpour, then indicated his quarters behind the church. 'Come inside for a moment,' he said. 'I've got something for you.'

Even before he could finish the sentence there came a sudden crack of thunder that was noticeably louder than those that had preceded it. At almost the same moment a jagged streak of lightning sliced through the cross that topped the spire. There was a grinding, splintery sound as it broke off and gracefully nose-dived to earth.

Instinctively Reed shoved Father Benedict aside, sending the old man sprawling. Reed, by contrast, remained where he was, staring up at the falling cross as if daring it to hit him.

Instead the cross stabbed into the ground where Father Benedict had just been standing.

The sound of thunder rumbled on across town. Reed stared at the inverted, still-quivering cross, then dimly remembered where he was and went to help Father Benedict up. Shaken and pale, the elderly priest crossed himself and then said: 'God bless you, Reed.'

'I doubt that,' slurred Reed.

'If you hadn't been here, I'd be dead.'

Reed shrugged. 'What can I say?' he asked. 'Call it Divine Intervention.'

* * *

Father Benedict led him into the church, down the aisle and past the altar toward the arched door that led into his office. To left and right lightning back-lit the clerestory — the row of small, stained-glass windows set high in the north and south walls, and for just the blinking of an eye Reed could have sworn he saw hunched, four-legged silhouettes blurring past them, on the outside.

Father Benedict's office was old-fashioned and homely, stuffed with books and paperwork. After the violence of the storm, it was an oasis of calm. The priest gestured toward an old Queen Anne wing chair and Reed dropped tiredly into it, watching suspiciously as Father Benedict went around to the business side of his untidy desk and opened a drawer.

He rummaged for a moment, then brought out a small velvet box which he handed to Reed. Reed took it as if it were a poisoned chalice.

'Where'd you get this?' he growled.

'Jacob Feldman. He told me to give it back to you. Said he never should have accepted it in the first place.'

'Why not? He did me a favor. I needed cash.'

'Reed, you don't pawn the Medal of Honor.'

Reed snorted. 'What else is it good for?'

Ignoring that the priest said cautiously: 'I can handle a small loan, if it'll help.'

Reed waved the offer away. 'Nah. I don't need money now. My disability check was late coming — '

'Well, promise me something, my friend. Next time you want to get liquored up, come to me first.'

'Why? So you can lay a sermon on me?'

'The way people keep moving away,'

Father Benedict replied ruefully, 'I could certainly use the practice.'

The priest's comment made Reed think about the town, how it was dying on its feet; how *all* of them, in one way or another, were dying on their feet. 'You got a pipeline to God, Father,' he said. 'Maybe it's time to call up a miracle.'

'I wish it were that easy.'

'Don't know until you try, I guess.' Reed held the box up and said: 'Thanks for this.' Then he got up, unsteadily, slipped the box into a pocket and limped back out into the storm.

★   ★   ★

In the darkened, poster-filled bedroom she shared with her sister Jalisa, thirteen year-old Skylar Lewis pulled the pillow tighter over her head. But it was no use — she could still hear her parents arguing downstairs.

I tell you, I got no place else to look!

I know, Ed, but you got to —

Got to what? Don't you get it, Momma? I'm wasting my time! I'm looking for something I don't ever stand a hope in hell of finding! Dammit, I'm looking for something that's not even out there anymore!

I know, Ed. I know it's tough. But you've got to keep trying.

You saying I'm not trying?

No —

That I'm not trying hard enough?

Now, you know that's not what I —

Twenty-two years I spent on that production line, probably the best twenty-two years I ever had in me, and what the hell've I got to show for it now? Nothing, that's what! I got no job, no prospects, and now my wife tells me I'm not trying hard enough to turn things around!

Ed! I never said that! I know you —

Forget it! Just . . . forget it!

Skylar hated to hear the anger in her father's voice. She hated that as much as she hated to hear the desperation in that of her mother as she tried to placate him. She wished she could be more like Jalisa, who was five years younger than her and didn't really understand just how bad things really were. Jalisa slept on the top bunk. And even through the pillow she could hear her sister's steady, even breathing and the occasional shift of the thin mattress against the wooden slats as she made herself more comfortable.

Although the Lewis house on Nugent Street had seen better days, pride still lived here. And that, Skylar thought, was the problem. It came hard to a man like her father to suddenly be rendered so helpless. He'd worked all his life, worked long, often anti-social hours to put food on the table and give his family better prospects than he'd ever had, and he'd taken justifiable pride in that.

Then they took his job away from him, the way they'd taken the jobs away from everyone at the plant, and all at once he became — in his own eyes at least — something that was somehow *less* than a man, And he hated it.

Skylar hated it too, the way things had changed.

They'd never been what you might call rich, or even middle class, but like Momma always said, they got by. Momma sent her two daughters to school neat and tidy and kept their modest home spotless. They were poor, but they were happy. They had each other, and that was the important thing.

Now their ever-shrinking finances made them even less than poor, and poverty was making them more and more unhappy.

Fighting tears, Skylar rolled over, her back to the door. She was exceptionally bright and to a point understood why recessions happened. But she couldn't help wondering why God allowed them. She and her folks were good people. Frankport was a good town. So why back everyone into a dark corner where they had no money, no happiness and no future? What did He hope to gain from *that?*

Downstairs a door slammed. Skylar guessed her father had stormed out and scrunched herself even tighter.

Momma had tried her best — *You got to keep hoping, Ed. You got to. Something'll turn up.*

But Skylar didn't really think Momma believed that any more than Poppa did. After all these months, Skylar hardly believed it herself.

4

On the way home Reed made one last stop at Bill's Liquor Store on Main. A couple of minutes later he stumbled back out onto the street with a fresh bottle of Seagram's VO in a paper bag. Soaked to the skin, he opened the bottle and took a generous pull at its contents. *There*, he thought vaguely. *That ought to scare off the chills*.

He splashed on through wind-ruffled puddles. Overhead, thunder sounded more like heavy artillery — the soundtrack to which he'd played out more than half his life.

And for just a moment then he was back in the sweating heat of eastern Afghanistan. It was late Saturday afternoon in the town that, since the USMC had moved in, had come to be called Combat Outpost Shahr — only this time the thunder was the explosion of a tarnished minivan driven by a Taliban suicide bomber.

The memory ended then as something quick and black splashed across his path, moving on all fours. He thought for a moment it was going to trip him, but then it was gone, swallowed by an alley's shadows.

In his drunken state he thought it might have been a stray dog.

It wasn't.

'Hey, soldier!'

He realized he was back on Main, with the wind and the rain slapping him. He blinked, peered around and saw her standing under the blue-roofed bus shelter on the other side of the road.

'What?' he yelled.

She stepped forward into the street-light. She had reddish-blonde hair, he saw, and looked tall and slim beneath her hooded, black vinyl raincoat. She had great legs that tapered down into red stiletto heels. 'Any idea when the next bus comes?'

He thought about that. It was a very good question. A very good question indeed. Now, if only he could come up with a halfway coherent answer . . .

He lurched forward and stumbled across the street toward her. 'Not till morning. 'Round six-thirty.'

'You sure?' she said as he joined her under the transparent shelter. 'The schedule said the buses run until midnight.'

'That was before all the layoffs.'

She moved to the molded plastic bench and sat down, huddling herself against the cold night. He looked at her. She was about half his age. But there was a worldliness to her that told him she could take care of herself, and he liked that.

'Use a bed for the night?' he asked impulsively.

Her expression was withering.

'No strings,' he added.

She made no reply.

He shrugged and took another pull at the bottle. 'Suit yourself.'

He turned and walked back out into the storm. He got about a dozen feet and then he heard her yell: 'Hey, soldier! Wait up!'

She jogged up to him, impractical red heels click-clacking against the sidewalk, a computer bag now hooked over one shoulder. 'Is it far?' she asked.

'Not really.'

She grinned. 'Then what are we waiting for?'

★   ★   ★

On the way to the forty-foot trailer he called home, she introduced herself as Lilith Adams. He said, 'Reed Devlin' and that was about all the conversation they had. A short while later they reached his trailer. It sat on blocks in a weed-strewn lot that was sheltered on two sides by trees on the southern edge of town. Parked out front was Reed's pride and joy: an old pickup that had twin chrome exhausts and a blower on the hood.

'Wow,' she said. 'You didn't tell me you lived at the Ritz.'

He grinned. 'Didn't want you to think I was bragging.'

Once they were inside and had the lights switched on she saw that the interior was nowhere near as messy as she'd expected it to be. Ignoring the dirty dishes in the sink she turned her attention to an old desktop computer that sat on the fold-down dining table. It had once been state-of-the-art but was now clunky and almost embarrassingly out-dated.

'I see you're keeping up with the times,' she said.

He chuckled. 'It does what I need it to.'

She accepted that with a shrug and looked about her. They were standing in a compact living area with fitted seats on three sides, a coffee table in the center of the burgundy carpet and some kind of wall unit that held a small plasma TV. To the right, beyond the galley kitchen, there was a series of sliding doors which she guessed opened onto a spare bedroom, shower, and master bedroom.

A headless toy Superman figure stood on top of the computer. About six inches tall, its head rested between its feet. A stack of old *Superman* comics were piled on a shelf above the TV. Beside them was a photograph of a sweetly-smiling young black girl.

Lilith stared fixedly at the photograph for a long time.

'Help yourself to the bed,' Reed said.

He peeled off his sodden jacket and hung it on a hook. 'I'm going to crash out here.'

'Think you'll sleep through this racket?' she asked, referring to the rain pounding on the roof.

'I will *now*,' he said, raising the bottle.

'Well, don't be shy, soldier. Pass it around.'

He did. She took a long swig and he was impressed when she didn't grimace.

'So, what brings you to Frankport?'

'Change of plans,' she said ruefully.

'Boyfriend?'

'I wish. I got mugged.'

'Jesus. What happened?'

'I was in Flint . . . standing outside the coffee shop where the Greyhound stops. Jerks knocked me down and grabbed my purse. I yelled for the cops but naturally they weren't around. I managed to hitch a ride here — '

'Whoa,' he said. 'If you're busted, how come you were waiting for a bus?'

'I bought some smokes at a diner. Still had the change from a twenty in my pocket. Figured I'd go as far as it would take me.'

'Where you headed — Detroit?'

Lilith nodded. 'Lucky I had my bag in a locker or they would've ripped off my laptop as well.' Her violet eyes settled briefly on the old desktop. 'Looks like you could use a new PC yourself.'

Reed waved the whiskey bottle at her. 'I need all my money for medicine.'

'Wondered what was keeping you here.' She took the bottle from him and took another pull. 'So now you know all about me. Your turn.'

He shrugged and flopped onto one of the seats. 'Not much to tell. I was born and raised here. Hard to believe, I know, but before the economy tanked the population was around fifty thousand. Now there's less than twenty.' He fixed her with a speculative look. 'Anyway, you haven't told me squat.'

'Well, what else do you want to know?'

'I don't know. What do you do for a living?'

'I'm an independent contractor.'

''Mean like you're a recruiter or something?'

'Kind of,' she said vaguely. 'I mean, I

am in the people business.'

She unbuttoned the raincoat and let it slip off her shoulders.

She was naked beneath it.

'You travel light.'

'I'm on a tight budget.' She came to him then, and almost before he knew it she was straddling his lap and grinding herself against him. Their mouths mashed together, tongues entwining, and because she tasted like everything that was tempting and taboo, it was impossible for him to resist her.

Something scampered along the top of the trailer roof.

Reed glanced up and Lilith said: 'Relax. It's just a bird.'

Maybe it was, at that. But he'd never known a bird make that much noise on the roof.

They kissed again and after a moment or so finally came up for air. Somehow he got to his feet with her still in his arms, her legs encircling his waist and crossed at the ankles in the small of his back. He lurched through the kitchen toward the master bedroom, slid the door open with one foot and then threw her down on the bed.

'Let's just get one thing straight first,' she said softly in the darkness.

He grinned at her silhouette. 'Lady, that one thing's already as straight as it's gonna get.'

'Not that,' she said, reaching for him. 'I'm no hooker. You got that?'

'Sure.'

'Good. Now get your ass down here. And remember this — I like to be on top.'

5

Diana Dixon hesitated briefly before rapping at the door. It was a little after eight a.m. and she'd just arrived at the skeleton-staffed newsroom of WDWC-TV in Sterling Heights, to find a message on her desk that said: *Jamie wants to see you*.

Diana's mouth immediately tightened. Well, that was just fine, she thought, because she wanted to see Jamie, too. In fact, she felt that a one-on-one with Jamie was long overdue.

She threw her bag under her chair, brushed at the shoulders of her powder-gray Anne Klein pantsuit jacket, which were still damp from her brisk jog across the rainy parking lot, and took the elevator to the second floor.

Tall and slim, with glossy black hair gathered in a pony tail at the nape of her neck, Diana was in fighting mood right until she came to Jamie's door and went

47

to knock. Then some of her determination crumbled, her thin, arched brows lowered fractionally above her large hazel eyes and she worried at her pouty lower lip with white, even teeth.

Why did he want to see her, anyway? As far as she was aware, no new or major stories had broken overnight, and there was nothing big coming up that they had to discuss. If it wasn't a new assignment, then what the hell was it?

Something told her that whatever it was, she wasn't going to like it.

But that was no surprise. So far her relationship with WDWC's new managing editor, Jamie Witt, had been rocky, to say the least. He was twenty-four years old, and as such eleven years Diana's junior. He'd come to WDWC straight from the American Broadcasting School in Oklahoma, full of big ideas to boost the station's shrinking ratings. Bernie Kolb, who owned WDWC, had been impressed with Witt's talk of demographics and local markets, the battle to win back the migratory Baby Boomers and the Nielsen estimates for the next season. Diana and the rest of the staff had decided to reserve judgment.

Diana, certainly, had been right to do so.

Jamie's first job had been to take her off the six o'clock news, which she'd co-anchored quite successfully for three years. No explanation was given; it was all part of Jamie's 'general retooling' scheme. So the woman who'd once regularly taken governors and lieutenant governors to task, who'd interviewed secretaries of state, state treasurers and once even a would-be president by the name of Obama, had suddenly found herself back on the road, interviewing the likes of 'Miss Pecan Pie' at yesterday's pizza-eating contest in Hamtramck, or covering the Polar Bears swim, as she was to do tomorrow lunch-time up in Frankport.

Her determination gaining the upper hand once more, she rapped briskly and a voice on the other side of the door said: 'Come.'

She pushed inside. Immediately her heels clicked intrusively against the Philippine mahajua wood floor Jamie had requested when he got hired. His office was large and airy, furnished in a style that was both ultra modern and extortionately expensive. The station might be failing, but apparently nothing was too good for Bernie Kolb's new *wunderkind*. The wall behind him was solid glass, speckled now with the breezy leftover drizzle from last night's storm.

Jamie sat behind an enormous desk, a handful of paperwork in one hand and a poised pen in the other. It looked so much like a pose that she was sure he'd struck it for effect the moment she'd knocked at the door.

In the cool morning light he looked even younger than he was. His sandy hair was short and thinning at the temples; his complexion pale; his eyes the same blue as his loosened-at-the-collar tie. But what people noticed first was his white lashes. They had been that way since birth. The only other color in his face came from brown freckles that spanned his button nose like a bridge.

'I got your message,' said Diana, closing the door behind her.

'So I see,' he replied, tapping his pen against his teeth. 'Take a load off your gams, as my father used to say.'

'You never had a father, Jamie,' she said, sitting. 'You just fell out of your mother's cookie cutter exactly as you are now.'

'Quit trying to get on my good side.' He swiveled around in his chair and refilled his cup from the coffee-maker beside him. 'Want some?'

'What I *want*,' she said, 'is to know why you sent for me.'

Some of his fake bonhomie immediately dissolved. 'Hey, don't get pissy. I may be a smart-ass college grad to you, but I'm still your boss.'

'Whatever.'

'I had a meeting with Mr. Kolb last night,' he said. 'We went back over the viewing figures for the last quarter and decided that in order to keep our younger viewers and bring those who've been deserting us back to the fold, we need to get more youthful faces up on the screen.'

She frowned suspiciously. 'Meaning . . . ?'

'Meaning we've identified our key

demographic as the sixteen to twenty-four year-olds. They're the people who matter to our advertisers, so that means they're the people who matter to *us*. If we're to win them back, we've got to give them presenters and reporters they can identify with.'

'Are you *firing* me?' she asked.

'No.'

'Jesus Christ, I'm only thirty-one!'

'Thirty-five,' Jamie corrected smugly, 'but who's counting, right?'

'For chrissakes, Jamie, you sound like something out of *Logan's Run!*'

'What can I say? It's a young person's world.'

'Oh, sure. And that's just fine when you're twenty-four. But you'll be thirty-five yourself one day, buster. See how you like it when *you're* put out to pasture!'

'No-one's putting you out to pasture,' he said with exaggerated patience. 'I know the value of . . . maturity. But the fact remains that you've had your time, Dixon. Our viewers want to see this year's younger, prettier model. And before you call me sexist, that goes for the guys as well — me included.'

'And you expect me to stand for it? I let you take me off the six o'clock news. I stood by while you passed out all the key assignments to Lisa and Brooke. What more do you want me to do?'

'I want you to coach our newest junior,' he said. 'Gillian Cox.'

'Who the fuck is Gillian Cox?'

'She'll be in later today. I'll introduce you.'

'Are you *seriously* asking me to teach my competition how to replace me? No fucking way — '

'Yes fucking way, Dixon!' he barked. 'That was an *order*, in case you didn't realize it. You'll show her the ropes or I'll show *you* the door.'

It was on the tip of her tongue to tell him to shove it, she was through. But he was right. Anyone above the age of thirty was considered a dinosaur now, in this business and almost every other. If she quit WDWC there were no guarantees she wouldn't face the same problems elsewhere.

'Was there anything else?' she asked tightly.

'No,' said Jamie, going back to his paperwork.

Too angry to say anymore, she left the office, feeling humiliated . . . and wondering how she could somehow wipe that smug grin off Jamie Witt's face.

They wanted viewers. All right — she'd *give* 'em viewers, enough viewers to make them sit up and notice. After all, she was a journalist, right? She'd find and break a story that would make Jamie Witt and Bernie Kolb realize that *she* was their star, not Gillian-Freaking-Cox.

Trouble was, where was she going to find that story?

★ ★ ★

Frankport.

Three teenage boys were passing the lot on which Reed Devlin's trailer stood when one of them, Rob Ainge, spotted a screech owl perched on the side-view mirror of Reed's old pickup.

It was a little after eight o'clock in the morning and the storm had left the air cool and bracing. Puddles lay everywhere, as still now as discarded mirrors reflecting the heavy, slate-colored sky.

Rob, short and stocky in his Fisherman parka and brown cord chinos, immediately came to a halt. He was fifteen, with a round, ruddy face beneath the mousy, bowl-shaped sweep of his Justin Bieber haircut. Acting purely on impulse he picked up a wet pebble and threw it at the owl.

By chance he hit the bird on the head. There was a sudden, squawky explosion of feathers and then the owl fell stiffly to the mud.

A moment of stunned silence followed. Then Rob's friend Todd Earl hissed: 'Shit, man! You *killed* it!'

'No way,' Rob said. 'I just stunned it.'

'It looks pretty dead to *me*,' said Eric Drake.

Todd, an ardent animal-lover since first grade, turned in a tight, agonized circle. 'You killed a fuckin' *bird*, man!'

Rob narrowed his eyes at the owl. 'I didn't *mean* to.'

'Well you fuckin' *did*, you stupid dork!'

Rob looked at his friends. Todd Earl

55

was tall and skinny, with a strange, elongated face that would stand him in good stead if he ever decided to become a funeral director. Eric was almost as tall, wiry but athletic, and the one who had the least problems scoring with girls at school.

Rob took another look at the bird. *Had he killed it?* He felt bad that he might have. But even as he splashed across the lot to make sure, he felt that he could still turn this thing around. If word of this got around school he'd become known as *that sick kid who kills birds*. But if he could instead become *the cool kid who threw a scare into that weirdo, Reed Devlin*, his stock would soar.

He looked down at the owl. It measured about ten inches from tip to tail, with reddish-brown plumage and a mottled white underbelly. Its round disc of a face appeared disconcertingly human.

The thing sure *looked* dead. He gingerly prodded it with the tip of his right boot. It offered no resistance. *Yup, dead, all right.*

He bent and picked it up — it was

surprisingly light — then turned back to his friends and forced a grin. 'Watch this, guys,' he stage-whispered.

With the owl in his hands he snuck up to the trailer door. The early morning was quiet and when he put an ear to the door he heard no sound within. Nervously chewing at his lower lip, he reached out and carefully turned the handle. *Yes!* As he'd suspected, Devlin had been too drunk to lock it.

While Todd and Eric looked on, he opened the door a crack. Almost at once he spotted Devlin slumped over his old computer keyboard, eyes closed, snoring softly.

Rob suppressed a snigger.

Careful to make every step as light as he could, he snuck into the trailer, tiptoed to the table and gently set the dead owl down next to Devlin's nose. See how he liked waking up to *that!*

As he turned to leave, however, Devlin's right foot shot out, tripping Rob and sending him sprawling.

Reed jumped up and towered over him. Years of wartime service had taught him to sleep light and wake instantly. His expression was tight with anger, and the anger intensified when he spotted the dead owl Rob had just planted beside him.

Grabbing the bird, he jabbed it in Rob's face. 'You little bastard! How'd you like to eat this for breakfast, huh?'

Almost in tears Rob started scrambling back toward the door. 'N-No, no, please, it was just a joke — '

Reed pursued him. 'So why aren't I laughing?'

'Please, mister . . . major . . . give me a break!' Rob heard himself whining and hated himself for it. 'I won't never mess with you again! Honest!'

Reed let him dangle for a few moments, then stepped back. 'Go on, get outta here!' he snapped. 'And take this with you!'

He hurled the dead owl at Rob. Instinctively Rob caught it, fumbled it, and bolted out the door.

As soon as he was back outside he threw the owl away and splashed across the lot in pursuit of his friends, who'd taken off at the first sound of Devlin's voice.

'*Wait up!*' he called. '*Wait up you fuckin' cowards!*'

He made it to the far side of the lot. Here, a small, dense wood covered a steep slope that screened Devlin's trailer from the rest of town. There was no sign of Todd, no sign of Eric. Rob swore again and slowed to a walk, his chest heaving as he entered the shadows of the wood.

Well, that was just fine, he decided as he calmed down. They'd done him a favor. Now they couldn't tell anyone what had happened here without having to admit that they'd run out on him. No one need ever know about it —

He frowned as he heard the beating of wings.

Coming closer.

He turned and looked up.

Shit.

The owl — the same owl Rob could have sworn he'd killed — dove down out of nowhere and slammed him in the face. Its talons raked his skin. He screamed and staggered back under the impact. He stumbled, tripped on an exposed root and went tumbling down the slope.

He rolled and bounced through the damp loam, wet, fallen leaves sticking to his arms, legs, and Justin Bieber hair. Finally he crashed against the trunk of a large hickory tree. The blow dazed him and he groaned. But there was no time for pain — that goddamn owl was intent on clawing out his eyes —

He got to his knees, fists clenched, spattered with mud, hair sticking out at odd angles.

There was no sign of the owl.

His shoulders dropped. *What a fucking morning*.

He heard a soft whisper of sound a few yards behind him, quickly twisted around, saw a bush shake as something brushed past it and then was gone.

Alarmed, Rob jumped up. 'Who's there?' he called fearfully.

There was no reply. Around him the wood seemed unnaturally silent, as if by entering it he had somehow left the rest of the world behind. He looked about him. The light was poor, his surroundings painted a dismal shade of sepia.

Behind him someone giggled.

He whirled around and again saw nothing but the empty woods.

'Who's there?' he yelled. 'Toddy? Eric?'

He heard the soft, quick tattoo of running feet behind him.

He spun, thought he saw the tail-end of . . . something . . . vanish behind the trunk of a tree five or six yards away.

Fuck this, he thought. *I'm out of here.*

He started back up the slope. He'd climbed it numerous times before but today it seemed to be steeper; and the farther he climbed, the steeper it got, until it was all he could do to put one foot in front of the other and keep his balance.

Footsteps raced up the slope behind him.

He turned and saw something pale duck behind a bush.

He faced front again, panicked now — and found himself staring straight into a pair of cold violet eyes.

Who the — ?

Aw-w Christ —

The newcomer shoved him hard in the

chest. As he fell backward he realized that someone else had crept up behind him and hunched down behind his legs so that he went straight over and spilled back down the slope.

It was as if the whole wood came to life then. As he rolled over and over he had a wild, kaleidoscopic view of ten of them, twenty, Jeez, at least a *hundred*, all just like the first one, breaking cover or dropping from the branches above, then spilling across the leaf-strew floor like a pack of hunting dogs, some running on two feet, others loping on all fours —

What are they?

They threw themselves at him before he could regain his feet. He screamed as they leapt on him and started jabbing, punching, scratching and clawing, all of them howling now, howling some weird, keening *trill* of pure animal pleasure.

As Rob's blood started to flow he screamed again.

He went on screaming for a very long time.

6

His head pounding from last night's drunk and his more recent encounter with — what was the kid's name, Angel? Ainge? — Reed splashed water on his face at the sink and dried himself off on his shirt. The coffee-maker burped. He took a mug from the stack of dirty dishes, rinsed it under the tap and then poured himself a cup, lacing it with a few precious drops from what remained of the previous night's bottle.

The bottle reminded him that he'd had company last night, a girl called Lilith. He walked unsteadily into the bedroom to say good morning but found only the empty bed, upon which sat Lilith's computer bag and a note.

Puzzled, Reed lurched to the bed and read the note. It said: *Thanks for the cheer. Give this to a needy child. Lilith.*

Reed opened the bag, took out a laptop and gave a low whistle of approval. It looked brand new, was bright red and thin as a magazine. He hefted it and was impressed by its lightness. His own desktop was an antique by comparison. But it was like an old friend, like comfortable slippers.

He returned the laptop to its bag, wandered back into the living room and dropped it on the couch just as someone outside tapped twice on the door.

Knowing who it was Reed called: 'Enter at your own risk.'

The door opened and the same sweetly-smiling black girl in the photograph — Skylar Lewis — entered. She was bundled up in old but clean winter clothes, and her big brown eyes peered at him from out of the eye-holes in the white woolen ski-mask that covered her face.

'Planning on pulling a heist?' he asked.

She giggled and tugged off the mask, then slipped out of her coat and gloves. She was a tall, slim girl with a bright, attractive face and black hair cut into a series of kinky twists. 'Momma keeps saying it's gonna snow,' she explained.

'So does Wilbur the Weatherman.'

'Wally.'

'Whatever.' He shrugged. 'What're you doing here anyway? Why aren't you at school?'

'It's Saturday, Mr. Devlin.'

'I told you to call me Reed.'

'Momma says I mustn't. Says I got to respect my elders.'

'Remind me to light a candle for her.'

'You gotta go to church 'fore you can do that,' she reminded him.

'Ah,' he said. 'I knew there was a catch.'

Skylar noticed the headless Superman figure and picked it up. 'Thought you said you were gonna fix this.'

'Put that down!' he snapped.

She flinched and he immediately regretted the outburst. She put the toy figure back where she'd found it and as she did so she noticed the almost-empty whisky bottle beside his coffee. 'Want me to fix you breakfast?'

'Don't be a smart-ass.'

'You got to eat, Mr. Devlin. Can't be drinking all your meals.'

'Yeah, yeah, yeah. Jesus, you're worse than a goddamn wife.'

'How would you know? You've never been married.'

'Trust me, scout, I know.' Without warning he felt the first stirrings of the restlessness that overshadowed his every day. 'I mean, you don't need to have fucking cancer to know you don't want it.'

Skylar shot him a chiding look and held out her hand.

He stared at her, said contritely: 'That just slipped out. I shouldn't have to pay for an innocent slip-up.'

She continued to hold out her hand, only this time she wiggled her fingers for emphasis. Reed rolled his eyes, grudgingly dug out some bills and gave her a dollar. She took it, opened her old purse and took out an envelope. He watched as she added his dollar to the money inside and then set the bag down.

'The starving children of Africa thank you,' she said.

He waved that away. 'Don't you know charity begins at home?'

'Not if you have a conscience.'

'Don't start on *that* again! 'Every seven

minutes a child dies in Africa.''

'It's *seconds*, not minutes,' she corrected. 'Every seven *seconds*, Mr. Devlin! If you're gonna be cynical about it, at least get your facts straight.'

Frustrated by his attitude, she went to the refrigerator. While she was inspecting the contents — which didn't take long because the fridge was more or less empty — Reed quickly dug out a twenty and stuffed it in her purse. By the time Skylar turned back to him he was innocently inspecting his fingernails as if he'd just discovered something of great interest beneath them.

'What have you been doing for food?' she asked him. Then as he shrugged: 'You promised me that you'd eat!'

'Hey, it's Lent. I'm not *supposed* to eat anything.'

'Excuse me, this is November, not February.'

He offered her a sour smile. 'No wonder I'm hungry.'

She gave him a long suffering look. 'Get your jacket,' she said. 'We're going shopping.'

* * *

They drove down to the local Busch's. Reed was slow to get out of the car and once in the supermarket dragged his heels behind Skylar as she wheeled a cart up and down the aisles. When she grabbed a box of raisin-bran he immediately shook his head. 'Cereal gives me the shits.'

'That's what it's supposed to do,' she said.

He had no comeback to that.

They stopped at the refrigerator case. She put a half-gallon of skim milk into the cart.

'I hate milk,' he said.

'It's good for your teeth and bones. Has lots of calcium.'

'What about cholesterol?' he argued belligerently. 'You want me to die from a stroke?'

'This is skim milk. Has only six milligrams of cholesterol per glass.'

He scowled at her. 'How the hell do you know all this stuff? I didn't know diddly-squat when I was your age.'

'You don't seem to know much more than that *now*.'

'Hey, what happened to respecting your elders?'

'It went by the wayside, as you're always saying.'

Again, he had no comeback.

'Besides,' she said, 'you didn't have Google.'

'Ah, yes,' he said sarcastically. 'How could one forget Google?'

They came to the liquor aisle. Skylar shook her head sadly as Reed put two bottles of Seagram's VO in the cart.

'I suppose that's strictly medicinal?'

'Took the words right out of my mouth.'

For a fleeting moment he saw the hurt in her eyes and tried to pretend that he wasn't responsible for it. It didn't work. The truth was, she was the only one who really cared whether he lived or died. He didn't know why. It was as if she'd woken up one day and decided to adopt him. But he had come to care about her too, perhaps for that very reason; she brought out in him a paternal side he'd never dreamed he possessed.

'So-o,' he said, unable to think of

69

anything else to say, ' — how's it going at school?'

She shrugged, not wanting to discuss it.

'Not so good, huh?'

'They've cut two more teachers and they're talking about going to a four-day school week.'

'Hah! Most kids would kill for that.'

'Not me.'

'Which makes you kind of weird.'

'Weird, how?'

'Like you're on a different runway.'

'I don't know what you're talking about.'

He searched for the right words. 'You know: screwed-up.'

'Why? 'Cause I want to learn?' She fell silent briefly. Then: 'Anyways, I'm not as screwed up as everybody says *you* are, so there.'

'Scout,' he said, 'you're not telling me anything I didn't already know.'

When they got back to the trailer Skylar fixed breakfast for the pair of them. She devoured hers, but the best Reed could manage was to prod everything around his plate.

When she'd first taken charge of him she used to lecture him about not eating. Now, she merely took his plate and scooped his uneaten food onto her plate.

'Too bad you weren't hungry,' he said as she wolfed everything down.

Unfazed, she used a crust to wipe her plate clean. 'You know, people would like you much better if you weren't always so sarcastic.'

'Then I'm winning the battle.'

'Why don't you want people to like you?'

'I don't know. Easier that way, I guess.'

'What's easier?'

He shot her a stern look. 'You're asking a lot of goddamn questions this morning.'

'If you don't ask, you don't learn, remember?'

The fact that she was quoting him shut him up.

'Why don't you want people to like you?' she asked presently.

He sighed. 'It's complicated.'

'I'm bright. You never know, I might just understand.'

'Being a loner . . . some people prefer it that way. It keeps things . . . simple. The

71

minute you invite other people into your life it gets . . . messy.'

'Not always.'

'No, not always. But I think it would get messy for me.'

'Why?'

'Scout, that's enough questions for one day.'

'If you say so.' Skylar got up and took their plates to the sink. Reed went and got a refill from the coffee-maker. While she wasn't looking, he picked up one of his newly-purchased whisky bottles and furtively added a splash to his coffee. She turned before he could finish, caught him in the act and glared reproachfully at him.

'I'm not your mother, you know. You don't have to sneak drinks behind my back.'

'My mother wouldn't have cared,' he said. 'Nor would she have said I was a lush.'

Irked, she put her hands on her hips. 'Excuse me, Mr. Devlin, I never said you were a lush. *You* did.'

'I don't remember that. When did I say that?'

'When I first met you, remember? I asked if you were one of those. You said one of what? I said a writer who drinks, and you said, no, I'm a lush who writes. In any case, you *do* know that alcohol is a depressant.'

'Another pearl of wisdom you found on Google?'

Ignoring his sarcasm, she said: 'How's your writing going, anyway?'

Reed sighed. Following his discharge he'd briefly entertained the idea of writing a book, a long, serious novel about man's reluctance to face his own mortality. It was going to be deep and significant, but it was also too much like hard work, so he'd settled instead for trying to write some lighter men's adventure novels. He was still trying.

'Oh, you know. One word follows the other . . . eventually.'

'Writer's block?'

'Doesn't exist,' he said.

'Get out.'

'It's true. Well, I guess it does exist. But only if you let it.'

'Deep,' she said.

'Now who's being sarcastic?'

She giggled. Just then the bag on the couch caught her eye. 'Hey, where'd you get the new computer?'

When he made no move to reply, she opened the bag and took out the laptop. Her eyes bugged with excitement. 'Wow!' she said, impressed. 'A new Deltium T-40.'

'If you say so.'

'Oh man, I'd *kill* for one of these.'

Reed watched her examine the hardware, secretly enjoying her happiness. 'What's the big deal?' he asked. 'You probably got one just like it at school.'

'Uh-uh. I don't even go to computer class no more.'

'*No* more?'

'Anymore.'

'Why not? I thought you said it was cool.'

'It is. But somebody ripped off the computers and the school can't afford to buy new ones. Only kids with their own laptops can take the class.'

'What kind of an asshole would steal computers from a middle school?'

'Same kind who'd set up phony websites to steal donations meant to feed the homeless in Haiti.'

He shook his head in disgust. 'It's a fucked-up world, all right.'

Before she could demand it, he whipped out a dollar bill, licked it and pasted it to her forehead.

She showed absolutely no reaction.

'Anyway,' he said, indicating the laptop, 'it's yours. Take it.'

She peeled the dollar bill from her forehead and added it to the others in her purse. 'Thanks, but you know I can't.'

'Why not? I'll never use it.'

'My dad wouldn't let me. He's always yelling about not accepting charity.'

'Who said anything about charity? I pay you, what, twenty bucks a week to clean up around here? Okay, then. Find out what second-hand laptops go for and you can work it off. Deal?'

He could tell by her expression that she thought her dad might go for that. 'Deal! Oh ma-annn . . . '

Impulsively she hugged him. He loved it but would never admit it. After enjoying it for a beat, he pushed her away and grumbled: 'Jesus, don't drool all over me.'

But she wasn't fooled for a single second. 'You know something, Mr. Devlin. I don't think you're as tough as you think you are.'

'Don't count on it.' He turned away from her, adding gruffly: 'Go on, get out of here.'

7

As soon as she left Reed felt a familiar mix of conflicting emotions. On the one hand he was happy that he'd seen her; on the other, he felt lonelier than ever once she was gone.

To chase away the loneliness he switched the TV on and reached for the bottle of Seagram's VO — then stopped. He didn't need Skylar to tell him that alcohol was a depressant. He knew that very well for himself. But somehow it eased — well, at least *dampened* — the depression that was in him whether he drank or not.

He knew that it would be nice to set the glass aside and say: *There. I resisted it for you, scout. Aren't you proud of me?* But this wasn't a feel-good movie and he wasn't that strong.

Instead he filled his glass and drank greedily.

He turned to the TV in time to catch a

news bulletin. The camera showed a stretch of blacktop beside a cornfield. It looked kind of familiar. A moment later he realized it should do — it was right outside town.

Police and State Troopers were talking to each other beside their parked cars while paramedics struggled to retrieve something from a waterlogged ditch.

A body.

Although the camerawork was shaky, there was no mistaking the black vinyl raincoat the corpse was wearing or her distinctive red stiletto-heeled pumps.

Reed felt his throat tighten. He leaned forward just as the reporter said: ' . . . the victim had no ID on her but police are hoping that fingerprints or dental records will identify her . . . '

Reed sat back, shook his head as if to clear it, his belly suddenly churning. That was Lilith! But . . . dead? When the hell did *that* happen, and how?

He stood up and set the glass down so hard that liquor slopped over the rim.

It *was* her, he was *sure* it was. But he knew he'd get no peace until he knew for certain one way or the other. Besides, unless anyone else came forward, he was the only one who could identify her.

He grabbed his jacket and headed out to the pickup.

* * *

The emergency services had packed up and gone by the time Reed parked his truck on the shoulder. Only a cordon of black and yellow *POLICE LINE DO NOT CROSS* tape marked the spot where the body — Lilith — had been found and recovered.

Still dazed, Reed climbed out. The early afternoon was watery and cold, with the threat of more rain. As an errant breeze ruffled the puddles he was struck by the almost-total quietness and isolation of the spot.

He walked over to the ditch, where the tape still fluttered in the wind. He looked at the skid marks still visible on the blacktop and wondered how this could have happened.

Lilith had spent the night with him,

and from what he remembered of it he knew it had been good. She'd been a passionate lover, but adamant about staying on top and calling all the shots.

With their passion finally spent, Reed had polished off another drink then drifted off to sleep. He wakened again a short time later and went to get a drink of water. Instead, he poured himself another shot. He barely tasted it. He yawned, so exhausted that he hadn't the energy to make it back to the bedroom. So flopping down in front of the computer, he decided to wait until the trailer stopped tilting around him and somehow drifted off to sleep.

It must have been while he was sleeping, he realized, that Lilith had walked out of his life and into her own death.

Behind him, he thought he heard someone laugh. He turned quickly. Standing in the cornfield he saw her — Lilith — and the shock was so great that he felt as if the ground was tipping beneath his feet.

Then he looked again and saw only a

scarecrow standing with its arms outstretched on its wooden frame. For some reason it reminded him of a crucifix. He thought: *Christ, maybe Skylar's right — maybe I do have to cut down on my drinking.*

But hard on the heels of that thought came another: His eyes might have played tricks on him, but he didn't think his ears had. He'd heard laughter, he was sure of it.

So who was out there, hiding from him in the field, who found the scene of a young girl's death so funny?

He received an answer almost immediately.

The silence was broken again, this time by a weird trilling sound. He looked around, just in time to see a screech owl flying toward the woods that bordered the far side of the field.

That's what he'd heard.

He took another look around. He wasn't even entirely sure why he'd come out here. Maybe he just wanted to see for himself where a girl he'd been intimate with had died hours later. Maybe he thought that would help him make sense of it or accept it if he saw the spot for himself.

It didn't.

He climbed into the pickup and drove back to town. Without realizing he drove overly fast and didn't stop again until he'd pulled up in front of the Frankport Police Department.

* * *

'So,' said Lieutenant Lyle Spader, his voice a businesslike baritone, 'they tell me you know the girl we took out of the ditch this morning.'

Reed hesitated. Earlier, having presented himself at the front desk and said he might have some information on their Jane Doe, he had been shown into a large, communal office that was sectioned off by a series of pale gray partitions and told to take a seat by a tall black policeman in a blue suit and burgundy tie. Lyle Spader — about forty, losing his hair, with wide-set, lazy-looking eyes with heavy lids — was one of the few detectives that had kept his job during the cutbacks.

'Well, did you or didn't you?' Spader said.

'Yeah.'

'She got a name?'

'If she's who I think she is, yeah — Lilith Adams.'

Spader started scribbling that on the pad in front of him. 'One *l* or two?' he asked without looking up.

'I didn't ask.'

'Did she say where she was from?'

'Uh-uh. Just that she was mugged in Flint and on her way to Detroit.'

Briefly he retold the rest of Lilith's story.

'So she basically spent the night with you, Major?'

'Yes.'

'Did you two — ?'

'Next question,' said Reed.

Spader shrugged. 'And she was gone when you woke up?'

'Uh-huh.'

The detective studied Reed for a moment, then opened a file, quickly rummaged through a sheaf of forms and statements until he came to a glossy eight-by-ten. He turned it around and slid it across the desk. The photograph showed a pale-faced girl with strawberry blonde hair, eyes closed, pale lips shut tight, stretched out on a stainless steel autopsy bench. 'Is this her?' he asked.

Reed stared at the image, swallowed, nodded.

'Major,' said Spader, 'I know all about you, of course. You're a genuine war hero, and there was a time when you were the golden boy of Frankport. But I gotta tell you something.'

'Which is . . . ?'

'Your story sucks.'

'Excuse me?'

'According to the Coroner's report, the girl you claim you spent the night with — the girl in this photograph — died sometime between eight and nine o'clock *last night.*'

'No way! Jesus, it was after nine when I picked her up at the bus stop.'

'Not if you believe the truck driver who says he knocked her down. He reported that he might have hit someone on that same stretch of highway — a woman in a shiny black raincoat — at about eight-fifteen. We logged the report at eight-forty-five.'

'Well, he's got the time screwed up. Lilith and I killed a bottle of VO till around midnight — '

'So you were pretty tanked up?'

Reed saw then just how far he'd really fallen. From town hero to town drunk in one easy lesson. 'Drunk or sober,' he said firmly, 'I don't imagine women who aren't there.'

'Then how do you explain her being dead in one place and alive in another, at the same time?'

'I can't.' Regretting his decision to report the matter in the first place, Reed said: 'We done here?'

'For now, Major. For now. But I got to tell you, I think we'll be talking again, me and you.'

8

As Diana Dixon drove into Frankport that Sunday morning she muttered: 'Christ, what a dump.'

Slumped in the passenger seat, Gary Chalmers, her regular cameraman, grinned at her. 'That's what you said last time.'

'Well, at least I'm consistent.'

'And a grouch.'

'Sorry.'

The last time she'd been here she'd been reporting on the closure of E&M Trucking and the loss of another 379 jobs. Now, as she drove her silver Toyota Camry along the ghost town-like street that had once been Main, then turned left in front of Frankport General in order to reach Weller Park, she saw the true cost of the recession and wondered briefly if this was the story she needed to re-establish her journalistic credentials.

Almost at once she decided against it. The American public was sick and tired of hearing about the recession. They knew the cost well enough and didn't need reminding. What she needed was a feel-good story, something that even the most cynical viewer couldn't resist. But feel-good stories — ninety percent of which were pure fabrications anyway — were ten-a-penny. Every local and national bulletin finished with one. It had become a tradition.

She needed something bigger, something better. But she certainly wasn't going to find anything here, covering the annual Polar Bear swim. She'd already mentally written her script: *Today the braver residents of Frankport, Michigan, made quite a splash as they took to the sub-zero waters of Lake Noquet, all in the name of charity. Upwards of fifty swimmers ranging in years from eight to eighty swam the quarter-mile between banks to raise money for yadda-yadda-yadda.*

The only reason she and Gary were here at all was to get footage of the event and perhaps a few talking heads. If they were lucky these people would get thirty seconds of fame on tonight's news.

She drove through the park gates and found a space in the lot. Even Weller Park itself, named in honor of Michigan's Nobel Prize-winning virologist Thomas Huckle Weller, seemed forlorn. On this damp, dreary Sunday morning it was shrouded in a fine, low mist that dripped from the sagging branches of skeletal red maple, white ash and pawpaw.

A crowd had gathered on the nearside bank of Lake Noquet. The locals were trying their hardest to create a carnival atmosphere, but it seemed to Diana that nothing could quite mask the sense of desperation that underlined everything about the town and its fragile survival.

She climbed out of the car and stretched. Gary, businesslike as usual, silently gathered his camcorder and sound equipment from the trunk. He was tall and skinny, with thick, wavy fair hair and skin that still bore acne-scars. At last he finished checking his gear and said: 'Okay. How do you want to do this?'

'I *don't*,' she said.

'All right, let me rephrase that. How does *Jamie* want us to do this?'

She stared off toward the lake. 'Get a few establishing shots, the crowd, the swimmers warming up for their ordeal, that kind of thing. There's got to be a dignitary or two around here. I'll go find them and then we can do a brief interview about the charity they're raising money for.'

Gary nodded and together they set off toward the lake.

★   ★   ★

Just like the rest of town, the public basketball court outside the projects had seen better days. There were no nets and the hoops were rusty. A warped chain-link fence, broken through in places, surrounded the court, where a handful of fourteen year-old boys were playing pickup basketball, their breath steaming in the chilly Sunday-morning air.

Today they'd been joined by a kid none of them had seen around before. He'd come out of nowhere and stood watching them play until they finally stopped and took notice of him. He looked to be about twelve and was small for his age. When Cameron Carlyle asked his name he'd told them Junior; that was all, just Junior.

He had a mop of red-fair hair and a pale face with deep-set violet eyes and a tight-lipped mouth. When they asked him where he'd come from he'd hooked a thumb back toward the depressing gray blur of the projects, half-obscured now by low mist. They guessed he must be new in town, which made him a *real* oddity. Most folks moved *out* of Frankport these days, not into it.

Cameron, who was lanky and had spiky black hair and a splayed nose, looked at the boys behind him. They looked at each other and then gave him a mixture of what-the-hell shrugs and nods. Cameron said: 'Okay, Junior. Let's see what you got.'

It turned out that Junior had plenty. In fact, he ran rings around them. It made no difference to him that they were taller, heavier, stronger or older. He was a blur as he took the ball from one end of the court to the other and left them all reeling in his wake.

After about ten minutes Cameron started to regret letting Junior play. It was a feeling he knew the others shared. But he thought he knew how to fix Junior. He deliberately drove for a layup and as he expected, Junior automatically tried to block him. Pulling no punches, Cameron knocked him sprawling, slam-dunked and then swaggered away, acknowledging the cheers of his friends with a series of emphatic, grinning nods.

Junior immediately leapt back to his feet and stalked after him. He looked furious now: the first emotion he'd shown all morning.

'Hey, man,' called Junior, his voice echoing flatly around the court. 'No fuckin' way that's a basket. You fouled me.'

Cameron turned back to face him while the others gathered around and grinned down at the indignant boy. 'Stop whining, bitch,' Cameron replied. 'Ain't no day been born that you can block me.'

His teammates started jeering at Junior.

'You don't like it, cut out,' Cameron added.

Junior scowled up at him. There was so

much hatred in his gaze that the jeers suddenly died and all at once it fell completely, uncomfortably quiet.

Junior reached slowly into his jacket pocket and pulled out a Boy Scout's utility knife. Unhurriedly he pulled out the four-inch steel blade.

Almost as one Cameron and his friends backed up a step, and Cameron raised both hands, palms out. 'Hey, man . . . '

'Yeah, man,' called Alton Blake, 'what you doin' with that shit?'

Junior said: 'Cutting out.'

No one saw him move. One minute he was standing a few feet away from Cameron, the next he was up close, and Cameron was bending forward over the blade that Junior had just plunged into his stomach.

Cameron's friends went crazy.

'Aw Christ — !'

'Judas-Fuckin'-Priest, did you see that?'

Cameron stared into Junior's face, into his peculiar violet eyes. Junior stared right back, his top lip tight and slightly folded under, like a snarl. He worked the blade around some more and Cameron's face twisted up and finally he screamed. Blood spattered the ground between his feet, and then the spell seemed to break.

'*What the fuck you doin', man —?*'

'*Ah hell, man, you killin' him!*'

Junior ripped the blade out of Cameron's stomach and Cameron, clutching the wound, trying to hold back the red tide that cascaded between his fingers, dropped as if in slow-motion to his knees. Junior watched Cameron's friends, apparently no longer interested in Cameron himself. They looked back at him, faces bleached with shock, wanting to run but rooted to the spot.

Junior grinned at them. And then —

So fast that they all flinched, he swept the blade around and straight into Cameron's neck. The blade severed the external jugular; and abruptly blood erupted from the wound, steaming in the cold air.

Some of Cameron's friends turned and ran. Two more bent over and threw up. Junior's mouth relaxed into a cold smile of approval. Then he refolded the blood-soaked blade, turned away and walked slowly off the court.

* * *

Had anyone thought to glance at the perimeter fence they would have seen a spiral of something that looked very much like cigarette smoke climbing slowly toward the leaden sky, while a young blonde woman in a black vinyl raincoat walked slowly away from the spot, her impractical red stilettos clicking rhythmically against the weed-littered sidewalk.

9

Sprawled across his bed — the same bed he'd shared with Lilith Adams on Friday night — Reed groaned as if in pain, his eyeballs scuttling back and forth beneath their twitching lids.

In his dreams he was back in Afghanistan. It was late Saturday afternoon again in Combat Outpost Shahr, and the tarnished van was pulling up outside the very place he'd been heading for — an alcohol-free bar called the Four Crowns, which was decked out like an English pub, right down to the beer mats and dart board. It was a popular meeting-place for off-duty soldiers and aid-workers, but in such an out-of-the-way place as Shahr not considered a prime target.

Big mistake.

There had been one split second when he noticed the vehicle — a green Toyota HiAce — and then the driver. The driver;

sweating hard, eyes glazed, mouth set, looking to neither left nor right, determined to engage no one in the narrow, dusty, crowded street.

Something inside Reed had wrenched and he'd thought: *VBIED*.

Vehicle-Borne Improvised Explosive Device.

A second later the van exploded.

* * *

Reed jerked awake and, certain he was going to puke, quickly rolled onto his side so that his head was hanging over the edge of the bed.

For what seemed like forever he stared down at the carpet and sucked greedily at the chilly air, feeling the sweat dribble down his face and drip off his eyebrows and nose. After a time the feeling passed, his heartbeat settled and he flopped back against the pillow and stared at the low gray ceiling.

Still so vivid . . .

The blast — the result of more than 750lbs of *Pentaerythritol tetranitrate*

— was so big that it had leveled close to fifty shops, killed twenty-seven Afghanis and wounded eighty US Marines.

Reed had been one of them.

When he'd regained consciousness he was sprawled on his back in the remains of an old souvenir shop and he could see the sky overhead because the roof had been vaporized.

In those first few moments he was so busy choking for air that he hadn't realized he'd gone deaf until his ears suddenly unplugged. Then there came a dizzying rush of sound — of people screaming in Dari and Pashto, Uzbek and Turkmen, of men bawling commands in English as they sought to bring order to chaos, of the distant wailing of sirens and the much-closer crackle of flames.

A wave of disappointment crushed him then, because if things had worked out differently —

But there was no time for self-pity. His men needed help.

He tried to rise. He was abruptly consumed by the worst pain he'd ever known, and teeth clenched, fell back onto his mattress of rubble. After a while the pain dulled and he was able to look down at the mess of his left leg.

At first he thought it had been blown off. There was so much blood and meat showing through his torn pants-leg it was hard to tell for sure. Then the world started spinning even faster. He threw up and passed out again. And the next time he regained consciousness he was in the local clinic and a nurse was telling him he'd been lucky. There'd been superficial damage to his ears, lungs and gastrointestinal tract, she said.

Oh yes, and he'd effectively lost his left knee.

While that was still sinking in she explained that the blast-wave had crushed the knee and damaged the ligaments and cartilage. Because the remaining fragments of the patella were so small the surgeons hadn't been able to use pins or wires to put it back together. Instead they'd somehow sutured it, and now his leg was stuck in a brace and would stay that way for at least the next four months.

He was shipped home and subjected to

a whole series of CRIs, MRIs and X-rays so the doctors could determine the full extent of his injury and then find a way to repair it. He went through what they called a period of 'prehabilitation' and then the damaged ligaments were replaced with parts of his hamstrings. A total knee replacement followed, but met with complications and he was left with a permanent limp and severely reduced quads that refused to respond to physical therapy.

Nine painful months later the army finally discharged him.

Now he got up, sighed and limped into the bathroom, where he washed his stubbly face with ice-cold water.

Sundays were always bad days. They reminded him that he'd lost his faith in God. And, what might be worse, in humanity too. But this particular Sunday had dragged even worse than usual. No matter how hard he'd tried to get away from it, he found himself thinking back over his Friday night with Lilith. He hadn't imagined her. If he had, then he'd imagined the bright red laptop she'd left behind her, and if he'd imagined that then so had Skylar.

So Lilith *had* been there.

But how could she have been somewhere else at exactly the same time, slammed dead by a truck and thrown into a rain-filled ditch? It didn't make sense.

Deciding to get out of the trailer for a while, he climbed into the pickup and drove down to Mulrooney's Irish Bar, one of the few bars still open in Frankport.

As soon as he entered the almost-empty place he recognized her — that woman from the TV, Doris — no, Diana Something-or-Other. She was sitting on a stool at the bar, drinking vodka and watching college hoops on the TV on the wall. A tall, skinny man with pocked skin was seated next to her, drinking a bottle of Miller Lite.

Reed went to the empty end of the bar and ordered a shot of Seagram's. The urge to swallow it in one was almost overpowering, but he forced himself to nurse it instead. He was still nursing it when the door opened again and Lieutenant Spader came inside.

The big, lazy-eyed cop stood in the

doorway until his eyes adjusted to the dimness. Then, when he spotted Reed, he came straight over, slid onto the neighboring stool and ordered a bottle of Blue Moon.

'Afternoon, Major,' he said in his distinctive low baritone. 'Knew I'd find you here. Spotted your pickup outside.'

'I can see why you made lieutenant,' said Reed, not bothering to look around.

Spader let the dig bounce off him. Reaching into his jacket, he took out a folded sheet of paper. He unfolded it, put it on the bar and slid it in front of Reed, saying: 'Check this out.'

Reed obeyed. It was a copy of a missing persons report that had been faxed through to Frankport PD from colleagues in Flint. It showed a photograph of an all-too-familiar strawberry blonde and gave her name as Marta D. Vann, age twenty-six, height five feet five inches, weight approximately a hundred and twenty-four pounds.

'I gave Flint PD your description of Lilith Adams, and this is what they came back with,' said Spader. 'This Marta D.

Vann disappeared four days ago. And that's not all.'

'Surprise me,' invited Reed.

'I think I will,' Spader said mildly. 'Her prints verify that she's the key suspect in a serial killing. She may be responsible for the deaths of twenty-two children.'

Reed *did* look at him then. 'You kidding?'

'I don't kid about murder, Major. The Department frowns on it.'

Reed stared at the fax again, trying to decide whether or not Marta D. Vann and Lilith Adams really were one and the same. The likeness was almost beyond doubt. *Almost.* But he wasn't entirely convinced.

'You know a kid named Rob Ainge?' Spader asked suddenly.

'I've seen him around.'

'Recently?'

'You say that like you already know the answer.'

'So answer the question.'

'The little shit snuck into my trailer yesterday morning and tried to leave a dead owl on my computer table.'

'What happened?'

'He thought I was asleep. I wasn't. I surprised him, threw him out, told him to take his damn' owl with him.'

'And what did he do?'

'He went.'

'Did you hit him?'

'No.'

'You sure?'

'Sure I'm sure. Why? Is he saying I did?'

Ignoring the question Spader said: 'Did you see which direction he went?'

'No. Why?'

''Cause he's disappeared, too.'

'*What?*'

'Gone missing. Vanished. As in, right off the face of the earth.'

Reed scowled, said softly: 'What's happening to this fuckin' town?'

'I don't know, Major. But whatever it is, I don't think we can blame it on the recession this time.'

He finished his beer, took back his fax and nodded goodbye. But before he could get halfway to the door Diana dropped down off her stool and intercepted him.

'Any developments in the Carlyle case yet, Lieutenant?' she asked.

'Not yet,' he replied flatly. He went to step around her, but she blocked his escape.

'No leads on the other boy, this Junior?'

'Not yet,' he repeated.

Diana frowned at him. 'Help me out here, Lieutenant. I have to file a story by six o'clock. So far all I've got is the name of the deceased and the name of the perp.'

'So call me at five-thirty and if we've scared up any new leads you'll get them then.'

She watched him leave. She and Gary had covered the Polar Bear swim and were just about to head back to Sterling Heights when Jamie Witt had called and told her about the murder of Cameron Carlyle. 'Cover it,' he finished. 'It's a youth story, so play up that angle. You know, pressure mounts on kids in no-hope town.'

It was a great angle — in principle. But it was easier said than done. They'd managed to get a few shots of the basketball court where a boy called Junior had stabbed a boy called Cameron, and Spader had obliged her by giving a perfunctory on-camera statement telling her that the matter was being given top priority by Frankport PD. They had some telephoto shots of the police carrying out door-to-door enquiries in the projects, but no one who actually lived there was willing to talk on-camera.

She went back to her stool and looked thoughtfully down the bar at Reed. She wondered who he was and what business Lieutenant Spader had had with him. Impulsively she picked up her drink, walked down the bar and slid up onto the same stool the lieutenant had recently vacated.

Bleary-eyed, Reed looked at her. 'You're Diana,' he said. And then, without warning, he finally had her last name: 'Dixon, right?' He frowned. 'Didn't you used to anchor the six o'clock news?'

She raised her drink in toast. 'Thanks for reminding me.'

'Loved your Polar Bear piece. Caught it on the two o'clock bulletin.'

She took a long, hard look at him, recognized his type and was tempted to say: *I'm surprised you were sober enough to watch it.* Instead she said: 'Actually, I'm staying over to report on the murder.'

'Murder? I thought it was an accident.'

'What was an accident?'

'The girl,' he said. 'Lilith. She got hit by a truck.'

'I'm talking about the boy,' Diana said.

'Ainge?'

'Cameron Carlyle,' she said, forcing herself to be patient with him. 'He got stabbed to death around noon today.'

'I don't know anything about that.'

'Isn't that what Lieutenant Spader wanted to talk to you about?'

'No.'

'What *did* he want to talk to you about?'

'Nothing that concerns you.'

'Who's Ainge?'

'Just a kid.'

'Did he see what happened to Cameron Carlyle?'

'Lady, I never even *heard* of Cameron Carlyle.'

'But Lieutenant Spader was interested in Ainge,' she said.

He nodded, muttered without realizing it: 'Sonofabitch disappeared.'

She studied him with new interest. 'Ainge is a kid who went missing?' she asked. 'When?'

'Yesterday morning, Now, no more fucking questions.'

Diana shrugged, got off the stool, took a card from her jacket pocket and passed it to him. 'Well, if you hear anything about Cameron, or you find out what happened to this other kid, Ainge . . . '

'Sure,' he said, and without really thinking about it he stuffed the card into his shirt pocket.

10

It was the crows that made the Officer
Jack Kelsey pull over and take a closer
look.

Until he noticed the way they'd
gathered on the tattered old scarecrow in
the cornfield it had been a pretty routine
Monday morning. But that's how it had
been just lately. There was a time when
Frankport had been lively and there was
always plenty to do. But as business after
business closed down and folks moved
away, so there was less and less to occupy
him.

'Course, having said that, there'd been
a missing persons report — some kid
who'd disappeared on Saturday morning
— and a fatal stabbing just yesterday
noon, but if things kept going the way
they were, Kelsey didn't know how long
the Department could keep running at
even its current reduced strength. Sooner
rather than later there were going to be

even more layoffs and he was afraid he might be one of them. For a career-minded guy with a wife and two young kids it was a scary prospect.

Then he noticed the way the crows had gathered on the scarecrow. They'd settled on its outstretched arms and a couple had even managed to balance on its side-tilted head, and . . . he didn't know, it just seemed wrong, somehow. Scarecrows were supposed to do just that — *scare crows* — not attract them.

He parked on the shoulder and got out. The scarecrow stood about thirty yards away, a ragged silhouette against the lowering sky. The crows were chattering to each other and pecking at it.

Frowning, Kelsey stepped into the muddy field and started toward it.

As he got closer he clapped his hands above his head. But the crows refused to scare and just carried on picking at the scarecrow.

He didn't know why, but it was then that he had the damnedest thought — that what he was actually witnessing here was some kind of feeding frenzy.

Something else struck him at the same moment — the isolation of this particular stretch of highway on this particular day. He felt suddenly alone and immediately chastised himself for letting his imagination run away with him.

He drew closer.

Closer.

And then he was close enough to see the scarecrow for what it really was.

'*Shit!*'

He reared back.

It was a man. At least he *thought* it was. The crows had done such a thorough job of stripping the flesh off its exposed face that it was hard to say for sure. It was . . . *someone* . . . and someone else had attached him to the scarecrow frame and let the birds do their worst.

They had.

Stomach twitching, Kelsey forced himself to go closer. He bent forward and peered up into what was left of the face. One eye had been plucked out of its socket. And through the streaks of blood that had worked their way down to its — *his* — chin, Kelsey could just about discern enough of a face to ID it.

Ah Jesus-fuckin'-Christ, he thought. *I think this is him, the missing kid.*

Rob Ainge.

* * *

'Today,' said Mrs. Winters, who ran Monroe Middle School's computer class, 'I want you to write a story about a school in which you're the principal. You can use *Freemind* to brainstorm your ideas, if you like.'

Skylar, one of the dozen or so seventh- and eighth-graders in the bright, echo-filled classroom, immediately raised her hand. 'What if we can't download *Freemind*?'

'You all use *Java*, and *Freemind* is written in *Java*, so you shouldn't have a problem,' said Mrs. Winters. 'Okay, get started, everyone . . . '

Skylar stared at her laptop screen. This was creative, exciting, and she couldn't wait to get started. She didn't even think she needed *Freemind* to help her organize her ideas. She knew exactly what she'd do if she were principal in her very own school.

Before she could get started, however, she had the weirdest feeling she was being watched. Sharon Crothers was sitting at the next desk across from her. Was she waiting to see what Skylar wrote? Skylar turned and looked at her.

But Sharon was already tapping away at her essay, staring intently at her keyboard.

Skylar was just about to turn her attention back to her own essay when she happened to glance through the classroom window and noticed a woman standing on the far side of the chain-link fence that separated the playground from the street. The woman was young and blonde, and she wore a shiny black vinyl raincoat belted around her narrow waist.

She was staring fixedly at Skylar through the curtain of cigarette smoke she'd just exhaled.

'Skylar?'

Skylar faced front again. 'Yes, Mrs. Winters?'

'Do you have a problem there?'

'No, Mrs. Winters.'

'Then let's see more *flair* and less *stare*, shall we?'

A titter ran through the room.

Mrs. Winters, a petite woman in her forties, with brown hair cut in a short, boyish style and large, black-rimmed glasses, went back to correcting paperwork. The room was filled with the industrious clicking of computer keys.

Skylar was in full flow when, without warning, her laptop froze.

She stared at the screen for a moment, frowning. The screen had gone a translucent white and her little circular blue timer started turning.

Impatiently she tried *Control/Alt/Delete*, but nothing happened. She didn't even get the options page. She waited a few moments longer. But when the computer remained locked she put up her hand and said: 'Mrs. Winters.'

'What is it, Skylar?'

'My computer's froze.'

'Try rebooting it. Sometimes that solves whatever problem caused the program to lock up in the first place.'

Skylar quickly logged off. As she waited for the laptop to reboot, she glanced back out the window. The woman in the black vinyl raincoat was no longer there. But she must have only just left, because Skylar saw a wisp of cigarette smoke curling in the air where she'd just been.

The laptop rebooted. She rubbed her finger over the cursor control pad but nothing happened. She tried again. Still nothing.

Then —

Slowly . . . slowly . . . a face began to appear on the computer screen, like an image gradually developing on photographic paper.

She frowned, more curious than alarmed, as it slowly took on features. He — it was definitely a man — was about thirty years old, with olive skin, short dark hair, a prominent nose and a short, dark beard. It wasn't a handsome face, but neither was it especially ugly. In fact, it was average in just about every respect; a face that would never stand out in a crowd.

Gradually the eyes began to take on

114

more detail, and Skylar realized they were the things that transformed him beyond all else. They were dark and gentle, filled with a seemingly endless well of compassion, understanding and wisdom.

They were not the eyes of an ordinary man.

Skylar felt almost hypnotized by them.

She rubbed the touchpad again, trying to make the cursor reappear. Again nothing happened. Yet the face on the screen, which in her mind she had already decided was some kind of fancy interactive wallpaper that had been activated by the reboot, seemed to shimmer. She watched it, so fascinated that it was a moment before she realized the lips were moving.

He was . . . *speaking*! And though no sound issued from the computer, *she could hear him as plain as if he were standing in front of her*.

What he said . . .

What he *said* . . .

. . . rocked her entire world.

She was so shocked in fact, that she fainted.

All around her the other children turned and watched, equally shocked, as Skylar gave a faint moan and then spilled loosely out of her chair onto the floor.

* * *

When she regained consciousness she was in the school nurse's office, wrapped in a blanket and stretched out on the examination table. As she sat up and anxiously looked around, Nurse Huey, a short, fat woman with a round face and dark skin, put a restraining hand on her shoulder.

''S'okay, child,' she said gently. 'You just had a little blackout, that's all.'

'Where's my laptop . . . ?' Skylar said, concerned.

'It's right here, hon'. Safe an' sound.'

Skylar relaxed a little when she saw it on the desk. Before she could say anymore, Nurse Huey poked a thermometer under her tongue. A few moments later she withdrew and examined it, then announced: 'Blood pressure's fine and her temp's normal.'

Skylar looked around and realized she

was addressing Principal Harrison, a thin, bookish man of about fifty, who was hovering beside the door like a worried wasp.

'Did you have breakfast this morning, Skylar?' he asked, coming closer.

'Yes, sir. Momma won't let Jalisa or me leave the house without eating our oatmeal.'

'And you've no idea what caused you to pass out?'

'Is that what I did?'

'Uh-huh. Do you know why that might have happened?'

'No, sir.'

'You're not on any medication we haven't been told about?'

'No, sir.'

Before Harrison could question her further there was a knock at the door and Skylar's mother, Lorena, burst into the room, followed by the principal's part-time secretary.

'What's wrong with my baby?' demanded Lorena.

'We're still trying to find out,' said Principal Harrison.

Lorena hurried to Skylar's side and hugged her. She was a big-hipped, still-handsome woman in her early forties, with straightened black hair and high cheekbones. 'Sweetheart, what's wrong?'

'Nothing, Momma,' Skylar said. But she wouldn't meet her mother's eyes, and Lorena noticed it.

'Come on, baby. You can tell me. Did something bad happen? Did someone try to hurt you?'

'Uh-uh.'

'Then . . . ?'

Unable to hold it back any longer, Skylar blurted: 'Momma, I saw *Jesus!*'

Silence. Then:

'W-What?'

'*Jesus*, Momma!'

'Jesus Christ?'

'Yes, Momma.' Now Skylar couldn't stop the words from coming. 'I saw him! His face! On my new laptop!'

Lorena forced herself not to jump to any conclusions, but it was hard. You didn't just go around seeing Jesus Christ on laptop computers! But what if Skylar had something wrong with her brain, something that had made it *seem* that way to her? She offered up a quick, fervent prayer that that wasn't the case.

Principal Harrison cleared his throat. 'Skylar, when you say you saw, ah, Jesus, do you mean you *thought* you saw him. You know, you *imagined* it? That it was a trick of the light?'

'No, sir, wasn't none of those things.'

He scowled, a sure sign he was stumped. 'Then it must have been a man *pretending* to be Jesus. I mean, anyone can say they're Jesus, but that doesn't mean they're really the son of God, right?'

'Excuse me,' Skylar said. 'He never said he was the son of God. He said he was Jesus of Nazareth, and he wanted me to trust him.'

'Maybe it's some kind of internet scam,' suggested Lorena. 'I mean, the first thing scam artists do is try to gain your trust, right?'

'Did he ask you to send him money?' Nurse Huey asked.

Skylar shook her head. 'He just told me to trust him.'

Lorena looked at her worriedly. She had to get her baby checked out. She wouldn't get any peace until she satisfied herself

119

that her girl was okay. 'I'm going to take her home now,' she said.

'Of course,' said Principal Harrison. 'And if she doesn't feel well tomorrow, keep her there.'

'I will.'

'One last thing,' said the principal as Lorena helped her daughter get down from the table. 'When this man spoke to you, Skylar, did he have an accent?'

'He didn't actually speak to me, sir.'

'But you just said — '

'He moved his lips like he was talking, but I couldn't hear him.'

'Then how do you know what he said?'

'I heard him in my mind. His voice . . . talking to me in a foreign language.'

'If it *was* foreign, child, how'd you understand him?'

'I don't know,' Skylar said, and suddenly it was all she could do not to cry. 'I just did.'

Looking at the faces all around her, she saw they didn't believe her.

'You can believe me or not,' she said defiantly. 'It don't matter to me. It was Jesus. I *know* it was.'

11

In his cluttered office at the back of St Mark's, Father Benedict listened patiently as Lorena told her story. At the end she said: 'First thing I was going to do was take her straight to see Dr. Ellis, but when she said this man had spoken to her in a foreign language and she seemed so *sure* about it . . . well, I thought you ought to know about it, Father. I mean, it wouldn't be the first time people've said God spoke to them.'

'I'll swear on the Bible if you want,' Skylar offered. 'I'm telling you exactly what happened.'

'That won't be necessary, child,' said the priest, thoughtfully stroking his mustache. He knew the Lewises well. They regularly worshipped at St. Mark's. Skylar was an exemplary child, bright, polite and as honest as fresh-baked bread. 'This foreign language, Skylar — would you recognize it if you heard it again?'

'I don't know, Father. Maybe.'

'*Ego sum Jesus Nazarenus, et volo te mini crede,*' he said. Then, in English: 'Was *that* it?'

'Uh-uh. Wasn't nothing like that.'

The priest pondered for a moment, then stared at the bright red laptop Skylar was hugging protectively. At last he reached a decision and picked up the phone. He punched in a number, said: 'Hello, Rabbi Koenig? It's Paul Benedict here. Yes, I'm fine, thank you. Listen, Rabbi — I wonder if I might drop by in a few minutes . . . and bring a very interesting young lady with an absolutely *intriguing* laptop computer along with me?'

* * *

Twenty minutes later they were all seated in the office of Rabbi Dovid Koenig, a small spartanly-furnished room in back of the Adath Israel Synagogue on Stanton Street. The Rabbi clasped his hands across his blotter, looked at the red computer on the desk before him and then smiled reassuringly at Skylar.

'I'm going to speak in Hebrew,' he told

her. 'I'm going to say exactly what you say Jesus said to you. Tell me if you recognize or understand what I'm saying.'

When he was finished, Skylar shook her head.

Rabbi Koenig repeated the sentence. Again Skylar shook her head.

'You're quite sure now?' Father Benedict said. 'Take your time. Think.'

Skylar hesitated, then said: 'It was sort of like that, but . . . I can write it down for you, if you like.'

'By all means,' said the rabbi, passing her a pad and a pen. 'Here.'

Koenig was tall and dark-featured, at thirty-two almost scandalously young to hold such a revered position in his community. Beneath his *hech* cap he had short, neatly-barbered mouse-brown hair and wore a thick, frizzy beard that fell to his sternum. He worked out, and even beneath his midnight-black robe it showed. When he spoke, his accent held an appealing hint of the exotic, his dark eyes a welcome glint of humor.

Skylar wrote quickly for a moment, then handed back the pad. Koenig frowned at it and then studied the girl with fresh interest. When he spoke again, it was in yet another dialect.

'*That's it!*' said Skylar excitedly. 'That's how it sounded.'

'That's Aramaic,' Koenig explained to Father Benedict and Lorena.

'Which is . . . ?' said Lorena.

'It's a Semetic sub-family which includes Canaanite languages like Phoenician and Hebrew.'

Father Benedict was almost scared to ask the question. 'Would Jesus have spoken it?' he asked softly.

'Absolutely,' Koenig replied. 'It was the day-to-day language of Israel in the Second Temple Period, 539 BCE to 70 CE.' To Skylar he said: 'Who taught you Aramaic, child?'

'No one,' she said. 'I've never even heard of it before.'

'Then how can you write it, baby?' asked Lorena.

'I dunno. I just can.'

'Write something else,' said Father Benedict.

'I can't. I can only write what Jesus tells me.'

Rabbi Koenig and Father Benedict swapped puzzled glances. The rabbi said: 'And you say this man shared the same coloring as me?'

'Yes, but his beard was shorter.'

'In other words, he looked like a typical Semite of that period,' mused Koenig. Addressing Father Benedict he said: 'You know, I've always found it fascinating how the Old Masters depicted Jesus as a fair-skinned, blue-eyed man with light reddish-brown hair, while his disciples described him as being very ordinary-looking . . . someone who wouldn't stand out in a crowd — a crowd, remember, made up of Romans and Israelites.'

'So what does this mean?' asked Lorena.

'I'm not sure,' Father Benedict replied honestly. 'But I do know one thing: that computer stays with me, under lock and key, until I speak to His Excellency Bishop Teal.'

'No way!' Skylar leapt up and dragged the laptop off the desk and tight to her chest. 'You can't have my laptop! I need it for school!'

'I'm sorry, my child,' the priest said.

'But if what you claim happened is true, this computer is potentially as religiously important as . . . as the Shroud of Turin.'

'Momma!'

'Hush, baby. Do as Father Benedict says. Give it to him.'

Skylar hesitated. They were going to take her laptop, her beautiful new laptop, and she felt instinctively that Jesus didn't want that. If she and the laptop were separated, then she and Jesus were separated, and she didn't think she could bear that.

Pretending as if she were going to hand the priest her laptop, she suddenly jumped back, startling everyone, and ran out before they could stop her.

'*Skylar!*'

'*No, child! Come back!*'

But Skylar had no intention of going back. Instead she sprinted from the synagogue, across the street, narrowly missing a car that squealed to a horn-honking stop, and disappeared into an alley opposite.

12

The Express Airways building just off Martin Street had been empty for the last eight months, ever since the company finally went out of business. With no other buyers interested in the combination warehouse-office building, it now stood abandoned, with a *TRESPASSERS WILL BE PROSECUTED* sign hanging crookedly from its sagging chain-link gates.

Skylar ducked through a hole cut in the fence and scurried up a rear fire escape to a door that had been forced open long before she'd discovered the place. Since then this had become her secret hideaway — at least she thought it was. She'd been coming here to get away from the constant bickering at home for a while now and hadn't been discovered yet.

Inside, she dodged through the first door she came to and closed it behind her. The small room had once been an office. It was now stripped bare. An old mattress lay in one corner, under a smeared window. She flopped down on it. Signs of her previous visits lay everywhere — empty Coke cans, Big Mac cartons, a half-eaten bag of Cheese Puffs.

Sitting with her back against the wall, she booted up the laptop and waited to see if Christ's face would appear again.

She heard something run across the floor directly above her.

Her head snapped up. She wondered if it might be a rat. Or maybe it was a person. Maybe someone else had discovered her hideaway.

She listened but heard no further movement. Instead she thought — *thought* — she heard someone out there . . . giggle.

She shuddered and told herself to stop imagining things.

At last the computer screen flickered to life and the image of Jesus Christ appeared exactly the way it had appeared the first time — like a photograph developing.

Skylar watched it take form, absolutely entranced. Once again the bearded man's mouth began to work, and in her mind she heard his voice say: *Invite me into your heart, my child, and I will save you.*

The face slowly faded.

Alarmed, Skylar said: 'No, don't go . . . Please, don't go.'

But the laptop screen went dark and she suddenly she felt as if she were the last person in the world.

She picked up and smoothed out a discarded Burger King napkin and used the pen Rabbi Koenig had given her to write down what Jesus had said. But how could she understand what he'd said without any knowledge at all of . . . what did the rabbi call it? Aramaic. How could she look at those words and know beyond any doubt that they said *Invite me into your heart, my child, and I will save you?*

And that in turn led her to a second question.

What do you need to save me from?

Without meaning to, or knowing why, she thought of whatever had run across the floor above her . . . and what had giggled.

* * *

The afternoon passed slowly, giving Skylar plenty of time to think. She knew she'd been wrong to run out on her momma, the priest and the rabbi. She'd always been raised to respect her elders, and now she felt ashamed of her behavior. But what else could she have done? They were going to take Jesus away from her, and she couldn't allow that. Of all the people in the world, for some reason, he had chosen to communicate through her. If she and the laptop were parted now, she might never get to understand why that was.

She curled up on the mattress and stared at the computer. Its presence was comforting. She closed her eyes and asked herself what made her so special that Jesus had chosen her. She couldn't think of a single reason, other than that she'd tried all her life to be good and to always do the right thing.

Was that enough? She didn't think so. There were plenty of people around like her, and a whole bunch much better than she was.

It was a mystery she was still pondering

when she drifted off to sleep.

Late afternoon brought with it shadows that grayed the room. The gloom was relieved only by the laptop screen, which suddenly began to glow eerily. In screen-saver mode, it showed an image that at first was all black. Then, over time, little dots of light began to speckle the inky blackness and grow larger. Planets and stars soon took shape, each one whirling past at dizzying speed. And then . . .

A naked woman came tumbling through space, a naked woman with long blonde hair and a flawless complexion and what appeared to be a shiny, near-black python curled around her.

Closer she came with every slow, sluggish revolution she made. Her hair floated and swirled as if she were under water. Her body was so perfectly propor-tioned that she would excite envy and lust in equal measure and from both sexes.

Surely she must have the face of an angel to match the rest of her.

She didn't.

As she came closer to the screen she looked up and her face was exactly the opposite of what it should have been.

The illusion of her perfection — and that's all it was, an illusion — did not carry to her face.

Her skin there was stippled with green and black scales, each about the size of a thumb-nail. They were in a constant state of flux, rippling from one side to the other, and from bottom to top, top to bottom, in some bizarre form of Mexican wave.

Her eyes were the same bright cherry red as arterial blood, faintly almond in shape and set above sharp ridges of bone. Her nose was long, her nostrils flared, her wide mouth at once sensual and infinitely terrifying. When she opened her mouth a thin, forked, impossibly long tongue uncoiled and writhed as if with a will of its own.

At last the creature came so close, its horrifying face filled the computer screen. Wrinkling back its lips, it bared its sharp-pointed teeth. As it did its breath caused a thin cloud of condensation on the screen. Its eyes glowed redly as it stared at Skylar.

On the mattress, the girl's face slowly contorted and grew similarly hideous. Her body writhed and twisted. Bones threatened to poke through her skin. A thin trickle of bile wormed from between her lips.

As Skylar convulsed a sound burst from her that filled the empty office and echoed throughout the abandoned warehouse —

The high, persistent *trill* of a screech owl.

The sound snapped her awake. She was slick with sweat, breathing so hard that she might just have run a marathon. Utterly confused, she looked around, wondering where she was, *who* she was. And again, as she heard the distant patter of feet scurrying across the floor above her, mingling with the bubbly giggling of what sounded like other children, she knew she was no longer alone. Frightened, she again wondered what Jesus was trying to save her from.

13

'Here you go, Father. This'll warm you up.'

Lorena came into the living room and set two cups of hot coffee down on the table between Father Benedict and her husband, Ed. The two men were seated across from each other before the fire.

'Thank you, my dear.' Father Benedict waited until Lorena joined her husband on the couch before adding: 'I must confess, I thought Skylar would have returned home by now.'

'So did I, Father.'

It was after seven, and Skylar had been missing practically the whole day.

'Has she ever stayed out like this before?'

'Never,' said Ed. 'She's a poster child for good behavior.'

'I still say we should call the police,' Lorena said.

Ed glared at her. 'And tell them what?

That Skylar ran off because she didn't want to give up her computer — a computer that, oh-by-the-way, she just happens to talk to Jesus on? Dammit, woman, we'd look like complete fools!'

He stood up and took a restless turn around the room. He was a big man, wide-shouldered and chunky, with a round, coffee-colored face and short black hair. To Father Benedict he said: 'You'll have to excuse me, Father, but I can't believe a man of God like yourself thinks that what Skylar claims is even possible.'

'Anything's possible, Ed. If I'd told you five years ago we'd have a black president, you would've had me committed.'

'Miracle as that was, Father, it's still a far cry from imagining you saw Jesus.'

'But what if she *didn't* imagine it?' Father Benedict said. 'Most people who meet her think Skylar is special. What if God feels the same way and chose to speak through her?'

'We should be so lucky.'

Benedict frowned. 'What do you mean?'

'If Skylar's not lying, you know how much we could get for that computer? Millions! *Tens* of millions! I mean, what's a miracle worth these days?'

'I prefer to think they're priceless,' Father Benedict said stiffly.

Ed waved one big hand dismissively. 'Don't get all bent out of shape, Father. This wouldn't only be a windfall for us. It'd be a huge boost for your congregation and a feather in your cap. Hell, you might even get an audience with the Pope.'

Embarrassed, Lorena put a hand on Ed's arm. 'Eddie, hush — '

But Ed Lewis was warming to the subject now, really seeing the full potential. 'It's true! Thousands of people would come from all over. Make pilgrimages here just like at Lourdes. Man, we'd be on every TV talk show in the country. The entire world. I can hear Oprah now, begging us to be her guests.'

'Ed, that's enough!' snapped Lorena. 'You're making something sacred sound sordid and commercial.'

'What's wrong with a little commercialism?' he said, sitting down again. 'A big fat miracle wouldn't only make us rich and famous, it'd put Frankport back on the map.'

Father Benedict tried to look suitably disapproving. But Bishop Teal's last warning still rung in his ears: *Unless you find a way to build up your congregation, you'll be asked to retire.*

And he couldn't deny that if things went the way Ed suggested, it would indeed be the answer to everyone's prayers.

★ ★ ★

As soon as he got back to St. Mark's he made a call to the bishop. But Bishop Teal's reaction to the news was as predictable as it was harsh.

'Listen to yourself, Paul! Good grief, I don't care what kind of student she is or how much she believes in God. She could be Joan of Arc and I'd *still* say she's either imagining things or her parents have put her up to it. My God, if the media thought we were even *suggesting* that a child saw Jesus on her computer, they'd crucify us!'

'I'm well aware of that, Your Excellency.'

137

Father Benedict kept his voice calm and placatory. 'And I understand your concern. Naturally, I'd never do anything to make the church a laughing stock. But I felt I should at least let you know what hap— Yes, yes, of course. I'll let you know as soon as I hear anything more substantial. Good night, Your Excellency.'

Benedict hung up and sighed. He understood completely that the church had to exercise restraint. With church attendance falling right across the world, such a claim as the one Skylar Lewis was making could easily be construed as a publicity stunt by an ever-cynical media and cause more harm than good. But Bishop Teal hadn't looked into Skylar's eyes the way he had; Bishop Teal hadn't heard the absolute honesty and conviction in her voice. And what about the girl's inexplicable understanding of Aramaic?

He looked at the crucifix on the wall and muttered: 'I hope you'll forgive me for what I'm about to do.'

And again he reached for the telephone.

* * *

Reed Devlin was almost but not quite falling-down drunk. He was in that place where the pain was subsiding to a dull throb, a place he had grown comfortable in and hated to leave. So when he heard a double-knock at the trailer door he yelled: 'Go to hell!'

There. That ought to chase them away.

But it didn't. The double knock came again, followed by a voice. 'Please . . . Mr. Devlin! Please let me in!'

Even in his cups Reed recognized Skylar's voice and immediately felt a stab of alarm. For a start, what was she doing out so late? And her voice . . . Christ, the kid sounded desperate.

Rising, he stumbled to the door and unlocked it. Skylar wrenched it open almost immediately and half-fell inside, her laptop hugged against her. She looked a complete mess, her hair straggly, the front of her clothes stained, possibly by puke.

She took a step forward, tottered and would have fallen if Reed hadn't caught her and lifted her effortlessly into his arms. He dragged the door shut and looked into her eyes. The terror he saw in them shocked him sober.

'Easy, now . . . easy . . . '

He set her down on one of the narrow fitted seats, poured her a splash of VO and passed it to her. 'Drink that down, kid. And then tell me what the hell's going on.'

Grudgingly she obeyed, choking as the whisky went down. 'Yuk!' she managed. 'H-How can you drink that awful stuff?'

'Never mind that,' he said. 'Just tell me what's wrong, scout.'

She looked directly into his eyes, her expression very serious. Around them the trailer was grave-quiet. Then, sometimes coherently, sometimes in a jumbled rush, she told him everything . . . beginning with the moment she'd first seen Jesus' face partway through Mrs. Winters's computer class.

Reed listened in silence until she was finished. Even then he didn't speak immediately. What the hell did you say to a story like that? At last he said: 'This

140

nightmare you had . . . '

'Wasn't a nightmare,' she corrected. 'It was real. I showed you the napkin. I can write it in Aramaic, too, if you want.'

'So what? People write in their sleep all the time. Write, walk, talk, act like they're wide awake and normal — '

'Excuse me, I was not asleep. And you'll never make me believe I was.'

'Okay, okay. Whatever it was, real or fantasy . . . has anything like it ever happened before?'

'Uh-uh. Never upchucked like that before either.'

'That could be food poisoning.'

'From what? I didn't eat anything different today than I always eat.'

'Stress, then. Reaction.' He eyed her critically. 'How do you feel now?'

'Fine, 'cept I'm sore all over. You know, like I fell downstairs or something.'

'Hm-mmm.'

She pointed to the computer bag on the couch, said: 'You gonna hide this for me or what?'

He ran his fingers through his short fair hair. 'Wouldn't it be easier all around if

141

you just let Father Benedict keep it for a few days? Hell, it's not like he's going to steal it. He's a priest, for God's sake.'

'No way. This is my laptop. I'm not giving it to anyone. *Ever.*' She gave him that careful look again. 'You *do* believe I saw Jesus again, don't you?'

'I believe you saw *something*,' he allowed. 'Maybe even a face. Was it Jesus Christ? I gotta chew on that for a while.' Catching the hurt in her expression he added quickly: 'Hey, I didn't say I *didn't* believe you.'

'But you don't. I can tell.'

'Look, what I believe doesn't matter. *You* believe it. That's enough.' He gestured to the computer. 'All right — I'll keep this for you. Now, let's get you home. Your folks must be worried out of their skulls.'

'All right. But you better drop me off before I get there. The less my folks know about your involvement in this, the better.'

Reed grinned. 'I won't argue with you there.'

14

The moment she entered the house her father was on her.

'Where the hell have you been, girl?' he yelled. 'Dammit, any moment we expected the police to call and say you'd been killed or worse!'

'What's worse'n being killed?' Skylar asked innocently.

'You'll find out, you keep smart-mouthing me like that!'

'Now, Eddie,' Lenora said from the doorway.

'Butt out of this,' he snapped. Then to Skylar: 'Now, where the hell you been? And why the hell did you run away from your Momma the way you did?'

'I was scared.'

'Why? 'Cause you was lyin' about that damn' computer? 'Cause you was afraid you'd get found out?'

'No, Poppa! I wouldn't lie about a thing like that! Not about Jesus — '

'Where *is* that computer, anyway?'

'Some kids stole it.'

'What kids?'

'I dunno. Just kids. Down on Front Street. They jumped me as I — '

Her father angrily grabbed her shoulders and shook her. 'Dammit, stop lying! I want that computer!'

'And I told you, I don't have it! You can believe me or not. It's the truth.'

Close to exploding, he pushed her toward the door. 'Go to your room!'

'But I ain't had supper yet.'

'Should've thought of that before you ran off. Now, get to bed!'

She went without further protest. Jalisa was already fast asleep in the top bunk. As Skylar undressed she smelled the soap flakes Mr. Devlin had used to wash the vomit off her clothes. He was a comfort. While she had him, she wasn't in this thing alone. And the thought of being in it turned her blood cold.

Slipping into her PJs, she knelt beside her bunk. Closing her eyes and clasping her hands she thought: *Please, Jesus, forgive me for lying. But if they take my* laptop, you won't be able to speak to me again. *And I know you can't want that to happen.*

★ ★ ★

The last of Father Benedict's guests arrived at a little after nine o'clock the following morning. As they took off their coats, nodded to each other and then made themselves comfortable in his office, the priest poured coffee and told them why he had asked them to come.

When he was finished Allan Reynolds, the small, white-haired, congenial editor of the Frankport *Dispatch* rubbed thoughtfully at his bearded jaw and said: 'Meaning no disrespect, Father, but . . . is this on the level?'

'I believe it is, yes.'

Jim Austin, the mayor, said: 'But what if it's not? What if this Lewis girl's just out to get her own reality show?'

He was a blustery, big-bellied man with a double-chin and glittering brown eyes. The others present — Councilwoman June Freeborn and Chief of Police Warren

Kennedy — chuckled dutifully.

'She's not like that, Jim,' said Father Benedict. 'I'll personally vouch for her honesty. Besides, how would she know Aramaic? Other than Rabbi Koenig, I doubt if there's another person in Frankport who speaks or writes it.'

He knew he wasn't telling them anything they hadn't already worked out for themselves. Chief Kennedy said: 'C'mon, Father. You know what you're asking us to believe?'

'A miracle, I know.' He paused for effect before saying softly: 'And couldn't we all use one right about now?'

'Amen,' said June Freeborn.

'Couldn't *Frankport* use one?'

'Double Amen to that,' Mayor Austin said.

'Well,' said Father Benedict, 'we've got one. I say we act on it.'

'What do you propose we do, Father?' asked Kennedy.

'*Believe*,' Father Benedict answered simply. 'Believe, and promote this miracle that the Lord has delivered to us for all it's worth.'

'Spread the word, you mean?' Reynolds said.

'Exactly. Far and wide. Newspapers, radio, television — the more people who hear about it, the better chance we have of attracting them here.'

'*And* the revenue they'll bring,' Austin said. 'We could sure use that. There isn't a soul in town who wouldn't kill for some extra business.'

'Of course,' Reynolds put in, 'that's assuming that everyone doesn't think we're a bunch of Jesus freaks.'

'I'm willing to take that chance,' June Fairborn said. 'And I bet everyone in my district will, too.'

'If it'll get me funding for more police officers, I'm in all the way,' said Kennedy.

'Me, too,' the mayor agreed. 'Come re-election time, a little 'nudge from Jesus' would suit me fine.' To Reynolds he added: 'Could boost your circulation, too, Al.'

'God knows we can use it, if you'll forgive the pun,' Reynolds admitted. 'But you're all taking one thing for granted — that the people and the media are actually going to *buy* it. Now, the people might, with a little persuasion, especially the Catholics. But the media? Forget it. We see this kind of thing all the time; the face of Jesus in the roots of an old asparagus fern, an image of the Virgin Mary in a plate-glass window, a kid in Des Moines who bleeds from the hands and feet. Set against that, what's so different about a little girl who claims to see Jesus on a computer screen?'

'Nevertheless,' Father Benedict said quietly, 'it's all we have. All that stands between us and ruination.'

'I say it's worth a shot,' Chief Kennedy said.

Though he tried not to let it show, Father Benedict felt a surge of excitement. Perhaps his prayers had been answered after all; perhaps Bishop Teal would see him in a new light after this and, frankly, get the hell off his case.

'We're agreed, then,' he said.

Mayor Austin looked around the room. There was something in the way he did it, in the way the room suddenly fell quiet, that reinforced the impression that they had all felt but were reluctant to admit, even to themselves — that they were conspirators here.

'Okay,' Mayor Austin said. 'Let's do it. But we keep this strictly between ourselves, agreed? If the media ever suspects we're pumping up a miracle for the sake of a buck, there won't be a sewer deep enough for us to crawl in.'

★ ★ ★

Diana and Gary were killing time in Elkin's Coffee Shop on Main, awaiting new developments in the murder of Rob Ainge and wondering if it was in any way connected with the stabbing of Cameron Carlyle, when Diana's cell rang. She pulled a face when she saw Jamie's name on the readout.

'If you're wondering what's happening here with the Carlyle killing,' she said by way of greeting, 'I'll tell you. The cops have got nothing to go on. Nobody knows the kid who did the stabbing. Nobody saw him before or after he did it, but something else has happened — '

She broke off suddenly, listened for a moment, then said: 'You are, of course, kidding.' Then: 'No, I don't want Gillian to go with me. Or Lisa or Brooke. I'm quite capable of interviewing a priest all by myself, thank-you-very-much.'

She ended the call and looked disgustedly at Gary. 'Fucking Jamie,' she said. 'Fucking prick. I swear he's trying to make me quit.'

'Another shitty assignment?'

'The shittiest. You ready for this? Says he got a call from the local newspaper, suggesting we go talk to a Father Benedict at St. Mark's.'

'About . . . ?'

'Some kid who has fireside chats with Jesus Christ on her computer.'

Gary rolled his eyes. 'Say *what?*'

'You heard,' she said, shaking her head in disbelief. 'What I can't figure out is how a kid comes up with this kind of crap.'

'From the internet,' said Gary. 'Where else?'

'Well, I still think it's a publicity stunt.'

'One way to find out,' he said.

15

Joel Dean said: 'Great. Just what I need — another laptop.'

He wasn't kidding. His ancient second-floor apartment on Angell Street was choked with them. And not just laptops — there were plenty of desktops, monitors and printers to keep them company, all in various stages of repair.

Reed opened the beer Joel had given him upon his arrival and gestured to Skylar's computer, which he'd just set down on Joel's tool-littered workbench. 'Apparently it was working fine yesterday, but when I tried to boot it up this morning there was no life in it.'

'So you thought you'd bring it to me,' said Dean.

A heavy-set man in his forties, with scraggly brown hair worn in a ponytail and a bushy beard, he was a far cry from the lean, tough-as-nails vet Reed had known in Afghanistan. He'd been solid muscle back then, and as close to fearless as it was possible to get.

Then they'd been sent to a contested area in Helmand with orders to disrupt insurgent activity there, and he'd lost both his legs to a roadside bomb. He'd been confined to a wheelchair ever since, and because of that he'd piled on the pounds.

'Only 'cause I couldn't think of anyone better,' Reed said.

'Yeah, yeah, yeah.' Joel made a quick visual inspection of the laptop. 'Nice machine. 'Course, it'll be obsolete about six months from now, but at the moment you've got yourself a top-of-the-range comp.' He glanced at Reed. 'You sure you want me to mess with this thing?'

'No, I want you to *fix* it.'

'It's just that . . . well, it's still under warranty, right? I mean, this hasn't been on the market for more than three, four months.'

'I *guess* it's under warranty.'

'What does that mean?'

'It means it was given to me.'

'Ah,' Joel said knowingly.

'It's not stolen,' said Reed, amending: 'well, not as far as I know. But I don't have any of the paperwork that goes with it.'

'All right. Let's open this baby up and see what ails her.'

Reed watched as Joel set to work. It was Reed who'd administered the rough-and-ready first aid that kept Joel alive until the Medevac could reach them. He sometimes wondered what Joel thought about that. He'd said thanks, that he owed Devlin, big-time. But it had seemed to Reed that his eyes had always said something else.

You kept me from dying so I could live like this?

Joel suddenly swore. The back was now off the computer, revealing the inside. Joel, looking into it, said frostily: 'Is this some kind of joke?'

'No. Why?'

Joel turned the computer around so Reed could see inside it. The laptop was just a shell — there were no physical components inside it at all.

'How do you expect it to start when

there's nothing in it *to* start?'

Reed had no answer. He said stupidly: 'It worked yesterday.'

'Well, don't ask me how. Did you see it working for yourself?'

'No. But — '

'Then I suggest someone is yanking your chain, ol' buddy.'

'No. Not possible.'

'Well, it's not possible that it could have worked. Unless . . . '

'What?'

'Unless it was switched for some reason. You say it was given to you?'

'Yeah, but then I gave it to someone else.'

'Who then gave it back because it stopped working?'

'Not exactly. It was working when she had it. It just didn't work for me.'

'Well, between it working for her and *not* working for you, someone's gotten into it and stripped it out.'

Reed looked doubtful. 'Could they have done that? I mean, this case looks like it came straight from the factory.'

'You got a better explanation?'

154

'I guess not.' Reed sighed. 'What I owe you?'

'A Bud and a game of chess next time we hook up at Mulrooney's.'

'You got it — so long as you promise not to whine when I kick your butt.'

'Dreamer.'

Joel quickly put the laptop back together, slipped it into its bag and gave it to Reed. Then he wheeled himself out of the apartment, past the out-of-order elevator until they came to the head of the stairs. Reed followed him, again feeling a stab of guilt for having saved Joel's life so he could be a virtual prisoner in an Aladdin's cave full of dead hardware.

'You ever decide to buy a new computer,' Joel said, 'come to me. I can save you a bundle.'

Reed nodded. 'See ya.'

Joel spun his chair around and wheeled himself back into his apartment.

He had just pushed the door shut behind him when he thought he heard a sound in the kitchen — the rattle of a disturbed plate, followed by a small, muffled sound that reminded him of a stifled giggle.

He frowned, called, 'Who's there?' and then wheeled himself into the small kitchen.

The kitchen was empty.

Better go easy on the weed, he told himself. *Or start using a better grade.*

He turned himself around and was about to return to his combination living room/workroom when he caught a flash of movement from out the corner of one eye. At the same time he heard a slapping kind of sound, like bare feet racing across a tile floor —

Before he could react something reared up behind him and clapped both hands over his ears, hard, momentarily deafening him. When he could hear again he heard a low, burbling kind of chuckle.

Swearing, Joel tried to turn himself around. But whoever or whatever was behind him grabbed hold of the wheelchair and propelled him back into the living room at a reckless pace.

Joel twisted at the waist, saying: 'Hey, what the fuck — ?'

But once in the living room whoever was behind him started spinning the chair round and round, faster and faster, so that the room started blurring and mixing into a sickening kaleidoscope of colors.

Joel felt vomit rise in his throat.

'*Quit* it! Please, whoever you are — '

They quit it.

And as they did so someone — something — else blurred around and ahead of him. Joel got a dizzying, indistinct view of it just as it opened the front door.

It turned and grinned at him.

It had blonde hair and uncanny violet eyes.

Then he was being shoved through the door and back out onto the landing, and the wheelchair was tilting a little on one wheel and then swinging left so that it was lined up with the head of the stairs.

Oh Christ no —

There was another giggle — it sounded like a *kid* — and then he was thrust forward, faster, faster, past the out-of-order elevator, ever faster —

'*No, no, no, please, NO — !*'

Joel grabbed for the spinning wheels

but the tread on the tires burned his skin off. He yelped and tried to grab them again, but by then it was too late.

He made a frantic grab for the banister rail but missed. A split-second later the wheelchair flew off the top step and into thin air, lurching forward and tipping down, Joel somehow tangled up in it so that man and chair together pitched over and over down the stairs . . .

* * *

Reed had just opened the curb-side door of his pickup when he heard the crash.

Already edgy, he threw the laptop onto the passenger seat and ran back into the apartment as fast as his bum leg would allow.

He burst into the lobby just as the wheelchair hit the bottom step and spilled Joel onto the tile floor. He went sprawling like the top half of a fat rag doll.

Reed was crouched over him even before Joel came to rest. One look at the angle at which his head hung limply told Reed his friend was already dead. But he still felt for a pulse and spoke Joel's name, praying he would answer.

He didn't.

Feeling as if he'd been kicked in the gut, Reed looked up the stairs as if expecting to find the reason Joel had plunged to his death. But the empty staircase offered no clue. Perplexed, Reed wondered what had happened. Had Joel remembered something, had some other theory about the empty laptop occur to him and come hurrying to the staircase to call him back so they could discuss it?

Unbidden, Reed thought about Lilith, and how she'd died after coming in contact with him. Now Joel had died while in Reed's company as well. Jesus! What was going on here?

What the *hell* was going on?

16

'Okay, Major,' Lieutenant Spader said, 'let's go through this again.'

They were standing outside Joel's apartment building and though the sun had finally come out it was still cold enough for the snow Skylar's mother had predicted. Joel's neighbours, having heard the crash, had called for an ambulance, and then for the cops. Reed had waited with the body until Joel was pronounced dead, then zipped into a bag and taken away.

Now Reed looked at the tall black lieutenant, said: 'I came over to visit. Joel and I served together in Afghanistan. We had a beer, shared a few memories.'

'And that's all?'

'What else could there have been?'

'That's what bugs me,' Spader said grimly. 'There's something going on here I don't like, Major. You tell me you slept with a woman at about the same time she was knocked down and killed outside town. That woman turns out to be suspect number one in a series of child killings. Next thing I know I get another child — well, he was fifteen, but technically he's still a minor — and he turns up dead as well.'

Reed's mouth went dry. 'You talking about Rob Ainge?'

'Yep. Found him yesterday morning. Hung up like a scarecrow close to where Marta Vann was killed.'

Reed remembered the scarecrow, wondered if it had been just that when he saw it on Saturday afternoon, or if he'd really been looking at the kid's corpse without knowing it.

'Kids,' Spader said suddenly. 'Aside from you, Major, *that's* the common denominator here. I had one kid kill another one on Sunday, and now we've got pretty much a whole class full of 'em from Monroe Middle, showing up at Frankport General, sick as pigs and showing all the signs of — '

He bit off suddenly.

'Of what?' asked Reed.

Spader turned him heavy-lidded eyes to him. 'Never mind,' he said.

Reed could think of nothing more to say. But he was thinking about another child from Monroe Middle, Skylar Lewis, who'd said she'd seen the face of Jesus on a computer that didn't have any innards.

'Am I through here now?' he asked abruptly.

'I guess so,' Spader said wearily. 'And for what it's worth, I'm sorry about your friend.'

'Me too, Lieutenant. I don't have many of them left.'

* * *

Mayor Jim Austin was optimistic only by profession.

No one had ever voted for a politician who said *you couldn't* or *you mustn't* or *we'd better not, just in case.* The electorate — and especially the block clubs, civic organizations and business associations — preferred folks who told them anything and everything was possible, that if you didn't try you'd never know. It was that *can-do* attitude that had helped Austin win three consecutive terms as mayor of Frankport.

Away from public life, however, Jim Austin was the kind of pessimist who ignored the silver lining and only ever saw the cloud; who refused to believe that the light at the end of the tunnel could be anything other than an oncoming train.

Now it was all he could do not to punch the wall outside Frankport General's fifth-floor Isolation Ward.

Wasn't it enough that their town — *his* town — was dying a slow death thanks to the recession? Wasn't it enough that their one chance to put the town back on its feet — the Lewis kid seeing Jesus on her computer — had generated little if any interest from the media? Wasn't it enough that two kids had been murdered over the past weekend? Judas priest, what more had to happen around here?

The answer was simple.

A fucking *plague*, that's what.

Again Austin looked through the observation window at the ward beyond. All of the beds were occupied by teenagers hooked up to a jumble of IVs and life-support machines. His eyes moved slowly, disbelievingly, from one child to another, always lingering on the red, inflamed sores that disfigured their faces and necks.

'My God,' he whispered. 'What's going *on* in there?'

Beside him the doctor in charge of the outbreak — and that's what it was, what it *had* to be — shook his head. 'We don't know yet. But more and more cases keep showing up. I'm afraid we're looking at an epidemic.'

Austin winced. 'For God's sake, take it easy with that kind of talk.' He chewed at the inside of his cheek for a moment. 'And you say they all come from the same computer class at Monroe?'

'Yes. That's the only common denominator we've found so far. But they all have siblings, Jim, so I'm sure this is just the beginning.' He fixed the mayor sternly and said: 'It's a hell of a thing, but unless I'm very much mistaken, I think we're looking at an outbreak of leprosy here.'

'*Leprosy?*'

'That's my early diagnosis.'

'*Here* — in the United States?'

'I know, I know.' The doctor shrugged. 'I'm still waiting for the results, Jim, but everything points to it.'

'I never knew leprosy worked this fast.'

'Usually it doesn't — which makes me wonder if we aren't looking at a new and altogether more aggressive strain.' He hesitated a moment, then said: 'We have to inform the CDC right away.'

'Here,' said Austin, immediately offering his cell. 'Go ahead. Call 'em. Be the one responsible for killing this town off once and for all.'

'Maybe you'd sooner we kill the kids, that it, Mr. Mayor?'

'Easy, now. Fighting among ourselves won't solve anything.'

'Sorry,' the doctor said. 'But I *have* to tell the CDC. I could lose my license if I don't.'

Austin tried hard to keep the desperation out of his tone and manner. 'Okay, okay, I understand. Sure, we gotta tell 'em. I know that. In fact I'd call 'em if you didn't. But . . . let me at least call an

165

emergency meeting first — talk things over with the city council.'

'What's that going to change?' asked the doctor. 'You think maybe one of them has a miracle cure hidden in his pocket?'

'Save your sarcasm, Tony. I have kids too, you know. You think I want to see one of them in there?' Again he looked at the teens in the ward and bit his lip, frightened by the thought alone.

'All right, tell you what,' said the doctor. 'You've got twenty-four hours to gather your talking heads together and then, no more stalling. I make the call.'

'Deal.'

* * *

In their living room on Nugent Street, Ed and Lorena sat on the couch, dressed in their Sunday best, with Skylar and Jalisa squeezed between them. That Skylar was there under protest was clear from her less-than-ecstatic expression.

Happy with the framing of his shot, Gary Chalmers said: 'Okay, C.B. — whenever you're ready.'

166

Diana squared her shoulders, cleared her throat and then held her microphone toward the family. 'So, Mr. Lewis, you *do* believe your daughter really saw Jesus Christ on her laptop?'

His eyes shuttling self-consciously between Diana and the camera, Ed said: 'My little girl's been raised to tell the truth, no matter what. If she says she saw the Lord and He spoke to her, then yes, I believe her.'

At Diana's urging, Skylar held up a sketch she'd been asked to draw of the face she'd described as Jesus. 'And this is the face you saw?' asked Diana.

Skylar nodded.

Diana turned to the camera: 'There you have it, folks. According to Skylar Deshone Lewis, you are looking at the face of Christ. Not the face we're accustomed to seeing, but Jesus' face as it might have really looked.'

She turned back to Skylar and said: 'Now, please tell our viewers exactly what Jesus said to you.'

Hesitantly Skylar said: 'He asked me to trust him.'

'What else?'

Before Skylar could reply, Ed said: 'Right now, that's all my daughter's willing to say.'

'So there *is* more?' said Diana.

'Much more. Skylar talks to Jesus all the time.'

Skylar frowned. It was the first she'd heard of it. 'Daddy — '

'Be quiet!' Turning back to Diana he said: 'This interview is over.'

Diana gestured for Gary to turn off the camera. 'What's the problem, Mr. Lewis? I thought you agreed to let — '

She broke off as the phone rang. Quickly Ed said to Lorena: 'Momma, answer that in the kitchen. Tell whoever it is to leave their number. I'll call 'em back.' As Lorena left the room he explained: 'It's been ringing off the hook since the crack of dawn.'

'I don't doubt it,' Diana said. 'Miracles don't come around that often.' Again she looked at Skylar. 'You're going to be famous overnight, kitten.'

'I don't wanna be famous — '

'I told you to button up,' snapped Ed.

168

'Now, you and your sister go in the kitchen.'

He waited for Skylar and Jalisa to leave, then confided to Diana: 'A producer in L.A. told me to name my price for the rights to this story.'

'Big surprise.'

'What're *you* offering?'

'We're just a local station, Mr. Lewis. We don't usually pay for stories.'

'Well, you want *this* story, you gotta pay for it,' he said. 'And don't give me that look. You'd do the same in my position.'

'What does Father Benedict have to say about this?'

'It ain't up to him.'

'I'd like to know anyway.'

'He doesn't like it,' Ed replied honestly. 'I don't like it myself. But if you expect me to pass up millions when I can't even feed my family, just so the Catholic Church can profit, then you're not being realistic. So what's your offer?'

'For an exclusive story?'

'You got it.'

'Let me make a call.'

'Make it quick,' Ed said. 'The price is

going up by the second.'

He waited until she and Gary had left the house and then went into the kitchen. Lorena was pouring Jalisa some chocolate milk. The carton ran out before her glass was full.

'Momma, you didn't fill it up,' whined Jalisa.

'That's all there is, honey,' Lorena said. To Ed she indicated the wall-phone. 'That was Principal Harrison. He was calling to see how — '

'That was Hollywood,' Ed said.

'What?'

'If anyone wants to know, that was Hollywood,' he repeated.

'I don't — '

'Starting from now, we only talk to the highest bidder, woman — even if we have to start to auction ourselves.' He frowned suddenly. 'Where's Skylar, anyway?'

'In her room, I guess.'

He went to the foot of the stairs and called: 'Skylar! Get yourself down here. Now!'

There was no response from upstairs.

'Skylar!'

Nothing.

He went upstairs, came back down a few moments later and told his wife: 'She ain't up there.' Not waiting for Lorena to reply, he ran outside, asking: 'Seen Skylar?'

Diana, on the front lawn and trying to get a signal on her mobile, shook her head. Gary did likewise. Ed hurried back into the house.

Father Benedict, having elected to wait outside in Diana's Camry during the interview, watched him go before deciding he could hold his silence no longer. Getting out of the car, he walked across the lawn to Diana. 'He's lying,' he said softly.

Diana stared at him, her search for a cell signal temporarily forgotten. 'Excuse me?'

'Jesus did not say anything else to Skylar.'

'How do you know?'

'Because she said so; to me, to her mother and to Rabbi Koenig. And she wouldn't lie to us.'

'Are you suggesting Mr. Lewis is trying

171

to hype things up to get more money?'

'I'm afraid so.' He leaned closer, saying: 'Now do you understand why I'm so anxious for that laptop to be in the hands of the church?'

'Sure. It's your meal ticket, too.'

Father Benedict's face hardened. 'Young lady, I find that most offensive.'

'Oh, come on, Father. I Googled you. Your parish has taken a big hit the last two years and like the rest of the country, you need a miracle to turn things around. A miracle like a young girl having a one-on-one with Jesus Christ. So why don't we all pull together? You're not the only one whose life is about to go in the toilet. Maybe if we team up, we can all end up wearing Armani.'

17

Skylar entered Elkin's on Main and slid unobtrusively into the booth opposite Reed, who was lingering glumly over coffee, still thinking about what had happened to Joel.

'Hi, scout. Want a Coke or something?'

'I want my *laptop*,' she said miserably.

'Is that why you called and asked to meet me here? You should have said — I'd have brought it with me.'

She shrugged. 'I don't want it yet.'

'Well, make your mind up. Do you or don't you?'

'I mean, I don't want it while there's still the chance they'll take it away from me.' She peered up at him, confided wretchedly: 'My dad wants me to lie, to say Jesus talks to me all the time! Says it'll make us zillionaires.'

'He's probably right.'

'I won't do it, Mr. Devlin.'

'Reed.'

'I won't do it,' she repeated as if she hadn't heard him. 'And I'm not going back there. You've got to hide me until this whole thing blows over.'

He raised his eyebrows. 'Are you nuts? Your folks would have the cops on me in a heartbeat.'

'Why?'

''Cause I gave you that lousy computer in the first place.'

She didn't argue the point, and that surprised him. Instead she got up as if to leave.

'Hey, where you going?'

'Somewhere nobody can find me.'

'Not so fast, scout. You run away, it'll only make things worse. Besides, how far do you suppose you'll get? Once they air that interview on the six o'clock news you're gonna be hotter than Lady Gaga.'

'I don't care. They'll never find me.'

'All right,' he said. 'Go. Hide out wherever you want.'

She frowned at him, trying to figure him out.

'Go on,' he said. 'See if I give a shit.'

'But — '

'If you don't trust me I don't want you around,' he said. 'Simple as that.'

'I *do* trust you.' She stared at him with eyes that were threatening to fill with tears. 'You gonna help me?' she whispered.

'Help you hide? No. But I *will* hang on to your computer. Since I gave it to you in the first place, I figure I owe you that. Now, come on. You can crash at my place for an hour or so and we'll try to figure out what to do next. Cool?'

'Cool.'

Reed put money for his check on the table and they left together. She climbed into the pickup beside him and he drove them slowly through town. He knew he was making a mistake by getting further involved in this mess, but what choice did he really have? Much as he hated to admit it, she was the only person that really mattered to him.

'What?' she said as he sighed wearily.

'It's that cereal you forced me to eat,' he said, straight-faced. 'My whole life's going down the toilet.'

Despite herself, Skylar giggled.

* * *

As soon as they reached Frankport's southern outskirts and turned one final corner they saw the police car parked outside Reed's trailer. One of the cops saw him coming — it was Jack Kelsey — and walked slowly out into the road with his right hand raised.

'Please,' Skylar begged. 'Don't stop!'

'Why not? I live here — '

'It's my dad, I bet! He's reported me missing and told the cops I'm here!'

Before Reed could stop her, she slid over to his seat and stamped her foot on the gas pedal. The powerful engine responded at once, gunning the truck forward and leaving a stench of burning rubber in its wake. Jack Kelsey quickly dived out of its way. Reed heard him swearing as they flashed by.

The pickup continued to fishtail madly and he had to fight the wheel to regain control. A glance in his rear-view mirror showed both cops now running out into the street, Kelsey pointing after them and yelling something obscene.

Reed tried to push Skylar back into the passenger seat but she fought him, stubbornly keeping her foot on the gas pedal. The leaf-strewn blacktop blurred along beneath them, rural Michigan sped past the windows in a series of vivid ambers and reds.

Only when they had skidded around a corner and were out of sight of the police did Skylar lift her foot and slide back onto her own seat.

'Nice job!' Reed said angrily. 'You just bought me six months in the can!'

'You said you'd help me,' she reminded.

'I said I'd hide your computer!' he corrected.

'Please, Mr. Devlin. I can't go home.'

He took another look in the rear-view mirror. There was no sign of pursuit yet, but that didn't mean it wasn't coming any second now. 'That makes two of us.' He fell silent for a moment, then shook his head. 'Aw, shit. Tighten your seatbelt, scout. Let's find someplace to lay low and work out what the fuck we do next.'

She held out her hand to him. 'That'll be a dollar.'

'At least let me get us the hell off this road first!' he replied.

Jaw set, Reed gunned the engine and the old, souped-up truck barreled on down the highway.

* * *

Though near-skeletal at this time of year, the woods were still beautiful. Those leaves that still clung to the trees were vibrant shades of copper and red, sienna and yellow; those that had already fallen carpeted the perpetually damp forest floor in the same bright colors. Reed kept the pickup bouncing and lurching over what passed for a trail until at last he turned the wheel hard left and they entered a clearing surrounded by bushes and shrubs.

Parking, he switched off the engine and for a while they just sat there, listening to the engine tick and tick and tick as it cooled. Around them beech and oak, maple and small hemlock trees stood sentinel. After a while curious chipmunks and an indifferent badger wandered by, while kingfishers and woodpeckers hopped inquisitively from branch to branch.

'When're we going back for my laptop?' Skylar asked at last.

'Your computer's the least of my problems right now,' he said, shooting her a stern look. 'I don't think you realize how much trouble I'm in. Running away from the cops is a felony.'

'Mean you could go to prison?'

'Make that 'will go to prison.''

'I'm sorry.'

'I'll be sure my lawyer mentions that to the judge.'

He'd said it without thinking, and didn't realize how harsh he'd sounded until Skylar started to cry.

'Aw, man,' he said awkwardly, 'don't do that . . . ' Impulsively he drew her to him and hugged her. 'Look, it wasn't all your fault. I didn't *have* to run from the cops.'

'B-But you did. And now they're gonna lock you up for it.'

'It might not come to that yet,' he said, not really believing himself.

That sat there for a while longer, deep in their own concerns. Dusk sent long shadows out across the forest floor and made the weak sunlight wink and flare through interlaced branches.

It grew colder. Even when he turned the heater on he could see their breath misting in the air. Seen in the growing darkness Skylar looked gray and exhausted.

At last Reed reached a decision and buckled his seatbelt back on.

'What are you gonna do?' Skylar asked.

'We can't stay here.'

'And you can't take me back!' she said, alarmed.

'I don't know *what* I'm gonna do yet,' he said wearily. 'But I need to think — and it's too damn' cold to do any thinking out here.'

18

He hated to go back into town. Even though it was late and the streets were largely deserted, he knew there'd be an APB out on them and if the police spotted him he couldn't risk attempting another getaway without making everything so much worse.

But he reached his destination without event, and pulled up outside a surprisingly well-kept two-story wood-frame house in an otherwise poor neighborhood.

Beside him Skylar had dozed off. He gently lifted her out of the truck and carried her up to the front door.

He couldn't reach the bell because his hands were full, so he kicked the door instead. A few moments later a light blinked on and he heard someone coming heavily down a flight of stairs.

The door opened to reveal what appeared to be a massively obese woman.

She was in full makeup, a mauve bathrobe and pink bunny slippers. She eyed Reed appreciatively for a moment then said throatily: 'Major! What a lovely surprise.'

Reed said: 'Can it, Jake. Let me get in off the street.'

'It's Jackie, in case you've forgotten,' Jake Rabowski said petulantly.

'Jake, Jackie, Josephine — I don't give a hoot what you're calling yourself now, just let us in!'

'Sure — sorry — come on in.' His voice deepening almost comically, he stepped back and allowed Reed to carry Skylar inside.

Reed went directly to Jake's living room and gently set her down on the sofa, where she finally began to wake up. Jake — Jackie, as he preferred to be called when he was in full make-up — followed them in, moving daintily for his immense bulk, a frown creasing his brow.

Reed introduced them. Jake said: 'Pleased to meet you, honey.'

'Same here,' said Skylar, adding: 'May I use your bathroom?'

'Sure. Top of the stairs, turn left, first door you come to.'

'Thanks.'

As soon as she'd left the room Jake hissed: 'What's going on, Major?'

Reed sighed, feeling everything catching up with him and wanting a drink he knew he couldn't have. 'What have you heard?' he asked wearily.

'According to the six o'clock news, you kidnapped that sweet little child.'

'*Kidnapped?* Ah, great. Just abso-fucking-lutely *great*. It was Skylar who came to me.'

'That doesn't matter. Right now you're a *major* with a *minor*.'

'Cute.'

Jake studied him with concern. 'What's the connection between you two, anyway?'

'One day she knocked on the door and asked if I needed someone to clean up. I didn't, but her old man's out of work and they needed every cent they could get.'

'A *beau geste*. How noble.'

'Up yours.'

Jake laughed briefly. 'And this so-called miracle she saw on her computer,' he said. 'How's that work?'

'Hell, I don't know. I've never known her to lie, but seeing Jesus on a laptop? Man, that's a stretch.'

'God works in mysterious ways . . . '

'Yeah? Well, He better have another miracle up His sleeve or I've got a date with the slammer.'

'Not if you get the right lawyer. No jury would convict a Medal of Honor winner of kidnapping.'

Skylar came back into the room. They didn't know how long she'd been outside or how much she'd heard, but she sounded determined when she said: 'I want you to take me home.'

'Little late for that,' Reed said.

'No, no,' she said, choking up. 'I'll tell them everything. Say it's all my fault. I'll even give Father Benedict my laptop.'

'Come here.'

She ran into Reed's outstretched arms. He hugged her tightly, with an emotion that he'd believed he no longer possessed. 'Calm down, scout. Everything's under control.'

'Please, Mr. Devlin. You gotta take me

home or you'll go to prison.'

'She's right, Major,' Jake agreed softly. 'You drag this out, buddy boy, you could face a long stretch.'

'What happened to that Medal-of-Honor speech you just gave me?'

'It just became extinct.'

'And you?' Reed said to Skylar. 'What about all your 'It's-my-computer-and-they-can't-have-it' talk?'

'I don't care about it anymore. I *hate* that stupid laptop. And I hate Jesus for asking me to trust him and to invite him into my heart then causing all this trouble.'

'No, you don't,' Reed said gently. 'You don't hate anyone. It's not in your nature.'

But he couldn't deny they were in a mess. He stepped back from Skylar and tried to think. She watched him through large, scared eyes. Reed reached into his pocket, took out a card, read it and thought some more. Then he finally turned back to Jake and said: 'Will you take Skylar home for me?'

'No!' Skylar protested. 'I don't wanna go without — '

He pressed his finger over her lips,

silencing her. 'Trust me on this, okay?' He raised one eyebrow to Jake. 'Will you do it?'

'Sure. And she's with me because — ?'

'I showed up with her, asked you to drive her home. You okay with that, scout?'

She nodded glumly.

'Good girl. Oh, and if anyone asks, the last time you saw your laptop it was with me.'

Again she nodded, teary-eyed.

He pecked her on the forehead and turned to Jake as if to say something. Instead he playfully yanked off Jake's wig, revealing a shaved head with a USMC insignia tattooed atop it. Jokingly kissing the tattoo, Reed replaced the wig so the long blonde ringlets were hopelessly askew and then hurried out.

Skylar gaped at Jake in shock.

With as much dignity as he could muster, Jake straightened his wig and said: 'Don't you just hate it when people violate you?'

19

Reed kept to the side roads and back alleys until he reached his trailer. Without stopping, he drove on in case the place was being watched, eventually pulling over about three hundred yards farther on. He limped back through the cold, snow-speckled night until he could scope the lot out.

When he was satisfied he had the lot all to himself he hurried through the darkness, unlocked the trailer and let himself inside. He closed the door behind him, then paused beneath the air vent that was located directly above the small cooker in the galley kitchen. Reaching up, he loosened the vent and pushed it aside. He then reached into the thin, exposed cavity between the ceiling and the roof and pulled Skylar's laptop from where he'd hidden it.

Replacing the vent, he was about to leave when an idea hit him. He turned and pulled the trash can from under the sink, rummaged through it, finally found what he was after — the note Lilith had left for him — and then ghosted back out into the night.

★   ★   ★

Diana was in her room at the Imperial Hotel, watching the late news without much real interest, when her cell rang. She picked it up, 'Yes?' then stiffened abruptly. 'When?' And then: 'I'll be there.'

★   ★   ★

She drove out of town until she reached the taped-off area where the body of Marta D. Vann had been discovered. She grimaced. Of all the places to pick! But maybe this guy Reed Devlin was playing mind-games with her, trying to spook her out. If so, he was succeeding.

She told herself she should have brought Gary along with her for back-up. But Devlin had told her to come alone, that it would be worth her while to do so.

As anxious and determined as ever to score her big story, Diana had agreed. But now, as she waited in the bitter darkness, her right hand strayed to her purse and the pepper spray that hung from her key-chain.

A thin carpet of fresh-fallen snow gave the moonlight a strange, artificial look, and she shivered. She peered through the windshield. As far as she could tell, she was all alone.

At last her eyes drifted to the dark cornfield. That was where they'd found the Ainge boy, where someone — apparently a number of perpetrators — had beaten him to death and then crucified him and left his corpse for the crows to feast on.

Quit thinking like that, she told herself. *You're a professional, dammit. Act like one.*

Without warning her cell buzzed. Startled, she jumped. But when she answered the call she was careful to keep her voice low and steady. 'Where are you?' she asked.

The answer came in the form of a soft

tap on the passenger-side window. She jumped again and twisted toward the face peering in at her — a face with a cell phone pressed to one ear.

Recovering, she hit the *unlock* button and Reed Devlin got in.

'Thanks for the heart attack,' she said sourly.

'Sorry. But I had to make sure you were alone.'

'So, what now?' she began; then seeing the red laptop: 'That the miracle maker?'

Reed nodded and set the computer down on his lap. She reached for it but he stopped her with a gesture. 'Let's just get something straight first, lady. I'm not a kidnapper. I didn't kidnap Skylar Lewis. She came to me for help and I tried to give it to her, but it kind of backfired.'

'Uh-huh.'

'You don't sound like you believe me.'

Diana shrugged. 'I've only got your word for it.'

'Not so. Right about now Skylar is back home explaining that I *didn't* kidnap her.' He could see by her expression that she didn't believe him. Indicating her cell, he said: 'Call her house. Talk to her yourself.'

For a moment she was tempted. But there was something about him that told her he was on the level. 'Okay,' she said carefully, 'for argument's sake let's say I believe you. That doesn't explain why you drove away from the cops. Or why you told Lieutenant Spader some cockamamie story about how you slept with a woman at the same time she was involved in a fatal RTA outside of town.'

'It was the truth.'

'And I'm supposed to believe you over a corpse, the guy who ran over her, and Lieutenant Spader, who-by-the-way has no reason to lie?'

'Who do you think gave me the computer?' Reed said.

'That's easy to say when she's dead.'

He dug Lilith's note from his pocket and gave it to her. Diana read: *Thanks for the cheer. Give this to a needy child. Lilith.*

'You or anybody could've written this.'

'But they didn't. Lilith did.'

'Who's Lilith, anyway? The dead girl's name was — '

'I know what Flint PD said her name was. She told me her name was Lilith. Lilith Adams. And with your help I think I can prove it.'

'How?'

'Fingerprints,' he said. 'Lilith's must be all over this note. If the police find a match with Marta Vann, that proves I'm telling the truth. And if I'm telling the truth about Lilith, I'm also telling the truth about this crazy laptop.'

Diana shifted a little. 'Let me get this straight. You want *me* to take this note to the police so they can check it for prints?'

'No, I want you to tell Spader that you've seen the note and that I'm willing to turn it over to him, so he can lift prints from it, *if* he'll get me off the hook on the kidnapping charge.'

She considered that. 'And in return I get . . . ?'

'To photograph the laptop and question me about Skylar and Lilith Adams.'

She pursed her lips. 'What makes you think Lieutenant Spader would listen to me?'

'That's your problem. Be persuasive.

But here's some more ammunition. First thing this morning I had this laptop checked out by a hacker buddy of mine, and guess what? It's empty inside.'

'*Empty?*'

'No hardware, no physical components — just an empty shell.'

'Then how's it work?'

'Good question. But that's not all.'

'Go on.'

'Right after he examined it, my buddy died.'

'*What?*'

Reed nodded. 'He lost both legs in a roadside bomb in Afghanistan. As I was leaving, he apparently lost control of his wheelchair — a wheelchair he's always handled like a stockcar — and ended up dead at the bottom of a flight of stairs.'

'You saying someone pushed him?'

'Sounds reasonable, right?'

'And you think there's a connection between the computer and his death?'

'You tell me.'

She thought for a while then said: 'Where are you staying?'

'Around.'

'Don't be coy. I just want to know where I can reach you.'

'You've got my number,' he said, and without another word let himself out of the car.

20

Reed waited until Diana had driven off, then picked his way across the cornfield to the stand of trees on its far side, where he'd left the pickup. He was halfway across the field when his cell rang.

'Yeah?'

Skylar whispered something that he didn't catch.

'I can't hear you. Speak up, scout.'

'I can't. I'm in my room now, supposed to be asleep. I don't want to wake Jalisa.'

'All right,' he said. 'Everything go according to plan?'

'After I told 'em what happened, Momma made Dad call the cops and he convinced them you didn't kidnap me. But they said 'cause I'm a minor, they still want to talk to you.'

'Don't worry, I'm working on that.'

'What about my laptop?'

'I got it with me.'

'Wish I had it. Now I can't go to computer class.'

'I'm sorry about that. But since you brought it up, I got a question for you: before the laptop froze or you saw the man's face — '

'Excuse me, Jesus' face.'

'Whatever. Before that happened, was it working all right?'

'Sure. Why?'

'Just wondered. I couldn't start it.'

He heard Skylar take a breath. Then she said: 'Momma's coming. I gotta go. Bye.'

★ ★ ★

In her room she ended the call, stuffed the cell under her pillow and pretended to be asleep. From the bunk above Jalisa said softly: 'Dad told you not to call Mr. Devlin.'

Skylar opened her eyes and stared up into the darkness. 'He won't know,' she hissed back, ''less you tell him.' She waited a moment, then asked: 'Are you gonna tell him?'

'Not if you give me your half of the chocolate milk.'

'There ain't any chocolate milk.'

'Next time Momma buys some, then.'

'All right,' Skylar whispered, relieved. 'But just this one time.'

Her mother's footsteps stopped outside the door. Both girls quickly feigned sleep. The door opened and their mother poked her head in. She saw that they were settled and quietly withdrew.

Skylar heaved a sigh of relief.

She then scratched at a rash of red swellings that had come up on her neck.

★   ★   ★

Deciding not to risk going back to Jake's place, Reed climbed into the pickup, pulled the blanket over himself and tried to sleep.

It was impossible. There was too much going on, too much that didn't make sense. All he could manage was a light doze; and it seemed that no sooner had he dozed off than his cell buzzed, jerking him back to full wakefulness.

It was Diana. She sounded tired — she should be, it was a little after one in the morning — but upbeat. She told him to come to her room at the Imperial, and gave him the number.

For a moment he wondered if he could really trust her. It would be easy for her to sell him out to the cops. Then they'd owe her one, and she stood to gain a bigger story from them than she'd get from him.

And yet he heard no sound of deception in her voice. Maybe she could be trusted after all. Maybe she sensed, however wrongly, that *he* was the story, and had decided to cooperate so that she would get it.

He told her he'd been there in twenty minutes.

He was.

He pulled up in the shadows behind the Imperial and entered the hotel through a fire door. The hotel was quiet and he encountered no one on his way to the third floor. He made his way directly to room 304 and knocked softly.

Diana opened the door almost immediately and let him in. As he looked around, automatically checking that they were alone, she handed him an already-poured glass of VO. He knew a brief moment of shame when he realized it was all he could do not to snatch it from her.

'Thought you could use this,' she said. She sat on the couch and raised her own glass in toast.

Somehow managing to resist his desperate urge to drink, Devlin eyed her suspiciously as he said: 'So what's the bad news?'

'There isn't any,' she said. 'It's all good. Spader's agreed to talk to the D.A.'s office — apparently he has an ally there — about dropping all charges against you.'

'What about Lilith's note?'

'Said to bring it in ASAP. Happy now?'

He raised his glass to her. But again did not drink.

'What's the scoop with you, Devlin?'

'No scoop.'

'Bullshit. First time I saw you I thought you were just another drunk. Then I Googled you and found out that you'd been awarded the Medal of Honor. Your

C.O. said he wasn't surprised you won it, just that you were still alive to accept it. Said you were either the bravest man he'd ever known or suicidal.' She cocked her head at him. 'Which is it?'

He forced a sour smile. 'You tell me.'

'No, no, you can't weasel out of it like that. It's your turn. What's more, I think I have a right. I mean, I've busted my ass tonight to get you off that kidnapping charge.'

'There's really nothing to tell.'

'No?'

He shrugged. He'd lived with it for so long he hardly knew what to say. Heaving a sigh, he said: 'If you must know, the men in my family have a history of strokes. My Dad died when he was thirty-eight, my brother when he was thirty-four, an uncle when he was forty-two.'

She looked at him as if trying to gauge whether or not he was joking. But one look into his eyes showed just how serious he was. 'So you figured you didn't have anything to lose, that it?'

'Just the opposite,' he said. 'I'm on borrowed time, Ms. Dixon; like a bomb just waiting to go off, if you prefer. If I'd stopped a bullet in Helmand or Fallujah or anyone of those other places, it would have been over for me. The waiting, I mean.'

'Look, I appreciate your fears. I really do. But you must be healthy or the Marines wouldn't have taken you. Right?'

'So far. But this is a disease that, when it comes, hits hard and fast.'

'Maybe it won't come,' she said. 'Ever.'

'Always that chance, I guess.'

Before she could pursue the subject his cell buzzed. He checked the caller ID, then said: 'Yes, Mr. Lewis . . . When? . . . Have you called 911? . . . Sure, I'll be right over.'

He ended the call and told Diana: 'Skylar's having some kind of seizure.'

21

By the time Reed's pickup squealed to a halt outside the Lewis house it sounded as if an angry demon had broken loose inside. Lorena was waiting for them at the front door, holding Jalisa in her arms. Reed's expression asked the question. Lorena said: 'Upstairs, first door on the — '

He'd already pushed past her and was limping as fast as he could up the stairs. Above him Skylar was screeching insanely. He hurried along the hallway and entered her room and saw Ed Lewis struggling to hold Skylar down on the bottom bunk. She was thrashing around, trying to bite and kick him, fighting his every attempt to calm her.

Reed saw at once that a series of angry-looking red blotches had broken out her skin. They resembled festering sores.

He went around Ed, dropped to his knees and tried to help restrain her. As soon as he touched her she stiffened, rigid as a corpse, her eyes rolled up in her head, bile oozed from her mouth and then she went limp and still.

Lorena, who'd followed him upstairs with Diana in tow, said from the doorway: 'Oh dear God, no . . . no, my poor baby . . . tell me she's not dead!'

'No, Momma,' Ed said shakily. But he and Reed continued to hold Skylar down for a few more seconds, fearful that her fit would return. When she remained limp, they finally let go of her.

'What happened?' Diana said.

Ed said in a choked voice: ''Bout ten minutes ago. Jalisa came running downstairs, screaming that Skylar was trying to kill herself. We didn't know what had gotten into her. She's never acted like this before.'

'Any epilepsy in your family?' asked Reed.

'I dunno. I never knew my folks. You think that's what it is — epilepsy?'

'Let's wait for the paramedics. They should know.' Reed pointed to the sores. 'When did these show up?'

'Tonight's the first time we noticed 'em.' He squinted at Reed. 'Didn't she have them when she was with you?'

Reed shook his head. 'Thanks for calling me,' he said.

'Didn't have no choice,' Ed replied. 'Skylar kept screaming your name and I got scared and — ' He broke off abruptly, suddenly asked: 'You got a girlfriend named Lilith?'

The name made Reed go cold. 'Why?'

'Skylar's been yelling her name, too.'

He glanced at Diana, then turned back to Ed: 'What else?'

'Threats. Truck-driver talk. I didn't know she even knew such words.'

'What's going on here, Mr. Devlin?' asked Lorena. 'I mean, what's really going on?'

'Yesterday, while Skylar was hiding out, she said something possessed her body. She couldn't tell me what, but said she lost all control and ended up puking on herself. I didn't know what to make of it. Figured maybe she had a fever or food poisoning or something — '

He stopped as heavy footsteps ascended

the stairs in a rush. A moment later two paramedics hurried in with Jalisa right behind them. Reed and Ed stood back to let them work. Skylar was still out of it, completely oblivious to the quick, basic checks they immediately started making.

'My daughter . . . she had some kind of fit and then fainted,' said Ed. He sounded absolutely bewildered.

'We'll check her out,' said the first paramedic. He pointed to the sores. 'How long she had these?'

'They're recent.'

Reed gently squeezed Ed's shoulder, said: 'How about some coffee?'

'No, I — '

Lorena said: 'Go on, Eddie. I'll stay with Skylar.'

Reluctantly, Ed allowed Reed to lead him out. When Diana tried to coax Jalisa from the room she refused to budge. 'I wanna see what they're gonna do to my sister,' she said.

'Maybe later, huh?'

'Okay,' Jalisa said reluctantly. 'But she better not die. She promised me I could have her chocolate milk.'

* ★ ★

As Ed made coffee Diana's cell buzzed.
She checked the caller ID, said, 'It's Spader,'
and then answered it. 'Lieutenant. What's
up?' She listened for a moment, then covered the cell and said: 'He wants to know
if I know where you are.'

Reed stuck his hand out, 'Let me talk
to him,' took the cell and said: 'This is
Reed Devlin . . . Uh-uh. I can't. Not now.
Skylar Lewis is sick and . . . I'm at their
house . . . Sure. I'll be here.'

He ended the call and returned the cell
to Diana. 'He's coming over with Rabbi
Koenig.'

'A rabbi? What's he bringing a rabbi
for?'

Beyond surprise now, Reed shook his
head. 'God knows.'

Lorena came downstairs to join them.
Ed looked at her expectantly, wanting to
get the news but half-terrified to hear
it. Lorena said tearfully: 'They're taking
her to the E.R. They say her pulse is
dangerously high and she's dehydrated.
And those sores on her face and neck?

206

Some of the other kids in her class have got 'em. They're all in hospital.'

As the paramedics came downstairs carrying Skylar on a gurney, Reed said quietly to Diana: 'I'm going with them.'

'What about — ?'

'If Spader wants me that badly, he can find me at the hospital.'

Diana nodded. As Ed and Lorena grabbed their coats and Lorena muttered something about leaving Jalisa with the neighbors, Jalisa said: 'Is Skylar gonna die?'

''Course not,' said Diana. 'Trust me. You're both going to be drinking chocolate milk till you're a hundred.'

22

Father Benedict's heavy sigh filled the cluttered office at the back of St. Mark's. He felt old and tired — and ashamed.

Rabbi Koenig had just called to say that the parents of a boy named Aaron Schneider had asked him to visit the child at Frankport General and say the *Mi Sheberakh*, an important Jewish prayer for those who are ill or recovering from illness, on his behalf. Apparently the boy, a thirteen year-old at Monroe Middle, had come down with some sort of illness and the word *leprosy* had been mentioned. A number of other children from the school had also contracted the disease.

'I thought perhaps you would like to add your prayers for them all, Father,' said the rabbi.

'Of course,' Father Benedict had assured him. But after he ended the call he had thought: *Leprosy? A disease of biblical times that is all but unknown here, in North America?*

Was such a thing possible?

Was it some sort of *punishment?*

He remembered that there had been something curiously fearful in Rabbi Koenig's voice.

Father Benedict himself had been struggling with his conscience ever since he had called the meeting with Mayor Austin and the others and tried to exploit the claims of young Skylar Lewis. He felt that he had been so blinded by what he stood to gain — the chance to stay on here at St. Mark's, to see his flock increase again and . . . yes, he had to confess it, to prove Bishop Teal wrong about him — that he had allowed his better judgment to be clouded.

Ever since then things had gone from bad to worse for the town. To begin with, apart from WDWC-TV the media had completely ignored or summarily dismissed Skylar's claims. Leaking it had gained the town nothing. And then there were the tragedies — the murder of two boys, the death of that poor legless man on Angell Street. Reed Devlin had apparently lost his mind and abducted Skylar and now this — leprosy!

Taken together, they all seemed too much like consequences to be ignored.

It dawned on him finally that God had been testing him all this time, and had found him wanting. Had he been stronger, perhaps, had he resisted the temptation to exploit that child — and a possible miracle — none of these things would have happened.

As redemption, he decided he would pray for the sick, as Rabbi Koenig had suggested, go to the hospital and do what he could to comfort the parents. But first, he had something else to do.

He looked at the telephone and played through his mind what he would say. *Yes, good evening, Your Excellency. I'm sorry to disturb you, but I've been thinking about what you said last week and, yes, I think perhaps it would be better for everyone if I stepped down and allowed new blood into St. Mark's. You were right — I'm not up to the task any longer. Perhaps I never truly was . . .*

210

Swallowing hard, he reached for the phone.

As he did, the phone slid away from him and dropped off the edge of the desk and fell to the floor.

Dumbstruck, Father Benedict turned his hand around and looked at his fingertips, because it had seemed that his hand had repelled the phone much as a magnet can repel iron filings.

An uneasiness that was purely instinctive flooded through him. He got up, went around the desk, picked up the phone and put it back on the desk. It sat there like something baleful.

He gritted his teeth. *Don't be a fool*, he chided himself. *You're letting your imagination run away with you*. But even so, when he reached for the phone again he did so like a man reaching for a primed bear-trap.

His fingertips were almost touching the phone when he heard a clatter off to his left. He whirled. At first he saw nothing — then he realized that the crucifix had fallen off the wall.

He crossed to it, picked it up and

checked it for damage. There was none. Christ was still pinned to the cross, his head, encircled by its crown of thorns, tilted slightly toward his left shoulder.

Father Benedict looked up at the wall, fully expecting to see that the nail he had tapped into the wall shortly after he had first come to St Mark's all those years ago had finally fallen out of the plaster.

It hadn't.

Then why had the crucifix . . . ?

Before he could finish the question, he became aware of something warm on his fingers and quickly looked down at the crucifix in his hand.

A thin red liquid was dribbling from Christ's palms and feet.

Blood?

No, surely n—

Then Christ's head slowly straightened, he looked up and his eyes — his *eyes!* — opened . . . and almost before Father Benedict realized it, they were staring at each other, he and the Christ figure.

In his younger days he had often wondered what it must have been like in Christ's company, to hear the soft modulation of his voice and the almost depthless wisdom of even his simplest sentence. And to look into his eyes, with their almost depthless knowledge and gentle compassion —

These eyes were not like that.

These eyes were cold and hard and violet, and there was something infinitely spiteful buried deep within them.

The Christ-figure opened its tiny mouth and more warm red liquid spilled down over the figure's chin and beard.

Terrified now, Father Benedict gasped, dropped the crucifix and backed away, his face a twisted grimace, his head shaking spastically, as if by denying the evidence of his eyes he could somehow regain a sense of the reality he had just lost.

He turned and stumbled for the door. Jerking it open he hurried into the church, almost tripping up the three steps to the chancel before he could drop to his knees before the life-size crucifix on the wall behind the altar.

He squeezed his eyes shut, pushed his hands together and his lips started working feverishly. *You are Christ, my*

Holy Father, my Tender God, my Great King, my Good Shepherd, my Only Master, my Best Helper, my Most Beautiful and my Beloved, my Living Bread, my Priest Forever, my Leader to my Country —

There was a noise behind him.

He turned and saw nothing.

He looked again.

This time he realized that someone was standing in the open doorway down at the far, dark-shadowed end of the aisle.

It was . . . no, it couldn't be, he really *was* losing his sanity . . . and yet it did appear to be —

— a naked woman with long blonde hair, a woman naked but for a snake — a python? — curled around her hips, hiding her vagina.

Someone spoke in his mind, a woman's voice, almost obscenely sensual.

You'll pay *for this.*

It was her! The girl he'd ejected from the church on the night of the storm! That's what she'd said to him — *You'll* pay *for this!*

The silence was so heavy now, as they

214

stared at each other, it felt almost like a physical force. Then a sudden gust of wind blew past the woman and swirled what appeared to be leaves — no, *feathers* — along the aisle until they reached the chancel. At last Father Benedict had the presence of mind to step hurriedly aside, watching with absolute bafflement as the feathers — reddish-brown and mottled-white, like those of a screech owl — spiraled and climbed and formed a whirring, blurring column.

There must have been millions of them.

Then one feather detached itself from the rest and flitted toward the life-size crucifix behind the altar.

Like a swarm of bees, the rest followed.

Soon they were coiling themselves around the marble Christ-figure, sticking to its lips, wedging into its nostrils, covering its sad, anguished eyes.

'No . . . ' murmured Father Benedict. Then, raising his voice to be heard above the howling gale: '*NO!*'

Slowly, the marble Christ began to writhe as if it were human and in agony as more and more feathers pasted themselves to it. In a moment feathers covered every inch of it — making look like it had been involved in a bizarre pillow-fight.

From the doorway, the naked woman with the python coiled around her began to laugh — a shrill, shrieking sound of merriment that was almost indistinguishable from that of a screech owl.

'*No!*' yelled Father Benedict. He hurried up the aisle, braving the storm-winds, raising his hands, palms out. '*No!*'

Abruptly the wind died, and those feathers not already stuck to the Christ figure started to float slowly to the floor.

'*Begone!*' Father Benedict said, advancing upon the woman in the doorway. '*In the name of the Lord Jesus Christ, by the power of his cross, his blood and his resurrection, I bind you Satan, the spirits, powers and forces of darkness, the nether world, and the evil forces of nature —* '

The woman threw her head back and laughed at him, his deliverance-prayer having no effect other than to amuse her. Her laugher echoed around the church,

216

shrill and harsh, and then she stepped to one side, turned her head so that she could look back out into the night, and he realized that she was not alone in her cackling; that others, clustered out there in the darkness, found his prayers equally pathetic.

They entered the church in a hopping, bounding, leaping rush, and all he could do was gawk at them and try to deny their existence by another vigorous shake of the head.

It was no good. They were *real*.

And they were hungry.

And, oh my God —

They were upon him.

23

Reed sat in a waiting room at the far end of the fifth-floor corridor. Skylar had been admitted to the E.R., then transferred to a bed in the isolation ward, where she was now hooked up to various life support systems. Ed and Lorena had been allowed to sit with her.

Tired beyond belief and desperately needing a drink, Reed felt as if he should offer up a prayer — more of a deal, really. *Look, You make Skylar well again and I'll try to be a better person. I'll quit the booze permanently if You —*

But why should God listen to him now? He'd never bothered to in the past.

Rising, Reed crossed the room, looked past his own haggard reflection at the dead town beyond. Around him the hospital was disconcertingly quiet. Over the past year a third of the wards had been closed permanently to save money, and staff had been reduced to the bare minimum. Given the choice, Frankport General was no longer the kind of hospital you wanted to be ill in.

He wished he had money. Then he could get Skylar transferred out of here. Oh, he had no doubt these people were doing everything they could, but they had limited resources and an Isolation Ward full of other, similarly sick kids right now.

He closed his eyes, his hands folded into fists at his sides and he thought: *Okay, here's the deal. Skylar's just a kid, got it? More than that, she's a good kid and she believes in You. You make her well again and I'll do whatever it takes to pay You back. You want me to be a missionary, go help those starving kids Skylar's always on about? You got it. You want me to renounce the demon drink and start going to church? I'll do it. I'll do whatever it takes, I swear it. Just make her well again.*

Footsteps sounded behind him. He turned, almost guiltily, expecting Ed and Lorena, or a nurse or doctor come to tell him Skylar was better, or worse, or that he might just as well go home because he couldn't do her any good here, not like this.

But it was Diana, Lieutenant Spader and Rabbi Koenig who entered the room. They all looked weary and grim, the rabbi especially, as he clutched an old book to his muscular chest.

'Sit down, Major,' Spader said. 'We need to powwow.'

Reed frowned. 'Is it about Skylar? Is she — ?'

'Just sit down, soldier. This is important.'

Reed dropped into a chair. The others joined him. Spader said: 'Go ahead, Rabbi. It's your huddle.'

Koenig placed the book on his lap. Reed tilted his head so that he could read the title. To his surprise it said *MESOPOTAMIAN DEMONS*. Koenig opened it to a place he'd marked earlier.

'Now, this is only speculation on my part, you understand,' he began self-consciously. 'But when I first heard that we might be dealing with an outbreak of leprosy here a lot of things started to make sense — at least to me.' He glanced down at the book. 'I'm going to read you something from a chapter entitled *Lilith*, known in Hebrew and Arabic as *Lilit*.' He paused a moment, then spoke again. ''Lilith is a female storm demon and thought to be a bearer of disease, illness, seizure and death. The figure of Lilith first appeared in a class of storm demons as *Lilitu*, in Sumer, circa 4000 BC. Later, she appears as a night demon in Jewish lore and as a screech owl in *Isaiah* 34:14 in the King James version of the Bible.'

Reed swapped uneasy looks with Diana and Spader. Even though he knew the answer, he still felt he had to ask the question. 'What are you guys trying to say?'

Spader said: 'I'm not completely sold on this, but it *is* kind of a coincidence. I mean, we've got a girl called Lilith who came to town in the worst storm anyone around here can remember. That was the same night she came into your life, Major, the night Father Benedict apparently found her or someone very much like her sleeping in his church and the night a truck driver named Ned Cross reported that he thought he might have hit a girl on the highway but couldn't find the body.'

'So?'

'I'm not finished yet,' Spader said. 'This guy Cross said he was attacked while he was looking for the body — by a screech owl.'

'Damn,' Reed said.

Spader nodded. 'Exactly. And it was a dead screech owl Rob Ainge tried to leave on your computer table, right?'

'Right.'

'And now *he's* dead.'

Diana looked at the rabbi and said: 'Tell Reed about Adam.'

'In ancient folklore, Lilith was the name of Adam's first wife,' said Koenig.

'I thought it was Eve?'

'God gave Eve to Adam to *replace* Lilith, who left him because she felt equal to Adam and wouldn't, uh . . . lie under him during sex.'

Spader, watching carefully, saw something in Reed's expression. 'That ring a bell with you?'

'I was thinking more about Lilith's last

name,' Reed said, not wanting to answer directly. '*Adams.*' To Koenig he added: 'Does the Lilith in the book have a last name?'

'No. But that's not unusual. Most demons in Mesopotamian mythology have only one name.'

'But in our world Lilith would need two. Could be she named herself Adams after Adam.'

'Makes sense,' said Diana. 'Show him the picture, Rabbi.'

The Rabbi turned to a page and showed it to Devlin. 'This is a famous painting of Lilith done in 1892 by a prominent British artist named John Collier.'

The painting showed a beautiful, long-haired, naked young woman with a python wrapped around her. Reed knew a moment of light-headedness. Then he said softly: 'Jesus. That's *her.*'

'There's another link,' said Spader. 'Since this Lilith or Marta Vann or whatever the hell she calls herself came to town, we've had two boys murdered and a whole bunch of kids confined to our

Isolation Ward with symptoms of leprosy. A particularly *aggressive* form of leprosy.'

'Which means . . . ?'

'Apparently Lilith's goal is to kill children,' Diana said.

'*What?*'

'She was cursed by God for leaving Adam,' Koenig said. 'As punishment she was commanded to give birth to a hundred demons every day and then kill them. To get her revenge, she supposedly roams the world at night, killing children of all ages.'

'Sounds like another Biblical legend to me.'

'Call it what you like,' said Koenig, 'but Lilith's name has been linked throughout history to the inexplicable deaths of babies, little kids and teenagers. A plague in Bulgaria, a children's school buried by a freak avalanche in Austria, a mass suicidal drowning in the Rhine — the list goes on and on. And Lilith is always there. Which is why, for centuries, people have called her the *Night Creature.*'

A thought suddenly struck Reed. 'She's going to kill Skylar!'

'She's going to kill *all* of our young people,' Koenig said.

'Sure, but Skylar in particular. She can't let her live.'

'Why not?'

'Don't you get it?' said Reed. 'If this is all on the level — and I have to admit, it does make a warped kind of sense — Skylar was supposed to be the carrier, the one who took the computer into school and infected all the kids with whatever kind of plague Lilith's unleashed.'

'Your point?' Koenig said.

'Then why did Skylar see the face of *Jesus* in the laptop? That couldn't have been part of Lilith's plan.'

Diana, whose own skepticism was gradually being eroded, thought she saw where this was going. 'Are you saying she chose the wrong girl?'

'I think I am,' Reed said. 'What if she mistakenly chose the one girl who was so . . . I don't know, *pure of heart* for want of a better phrase . . . a girl who could somehow channel the forces of *Good* through that damn' laptop?'

'Then she'd have to eliminate Skylar as

a matter of urgency,' Diana said. 'Before she could use the laptop against Lilith and bring the forces of Good into play.' She shook her head, muttered: 'I can't even believe I just said that. This is all frigging nonsense — !'

'You don't believe that any more than I do,' said Reed. 'This isn't something we can just dismiss, it's not something we can *afford* to dismiss! Ever since last Friday night this town has literally been going to hell. We've got a girl who sees Christ in a laptop that doesn't have any innards. We've got the guy who opened it up and examined it who died in a freak accident just a few minutes later. We've had one boy go missing and turn up dead in a cornfield. We've had a kid no one's ever seen before stab another one to death over a stupid disagreement. And right next door we've got Christ knows how many kids dying from what appears to be leprosy. Coincidence? I don't think so.'

He stood up. Spader said: 'Hold on, Major — where do you think you're going?'

Not bothering to reply he limped from the room and Diana followed him. Spader and the rabbi exchanged a look and Koenig said softly: 'I'm inclined to think Major Devlin might be right.'

Reed hurried to the Isolation Ward and was surprised to find Ed and Lorena waiting beside the nurse's station. 'What's happened?' he demanded.

'Relax,' Ed said wearily. 'The doctor took her to be X-rayed. She was worried that Skylar might have injured herself internally during the seizure.'

'*She?* I thought the doctor on duty was a man, Dr. Goldwing?'

'Dr. Eden isn't part of the hospital staff. She's some kind of specialist,' said Lorena.

'*Eden?*' Urgently Reed said: 'Was she young? Pretty? Long blonde hair?'

Lorena shrugged. 'I don't remember. She was in scrubs and wore one of those surgery caps — '

'I remember,' Ed said. 'She was pretty and her hair was definitely blonde. Why?'

'Eden,' Diana said as Spader and Koenig hurried up. 'As in the Garden of?'

Reed grabbed Ed's arm. 'Which way did she take Skylar?'

'I don't — '

'*Which way, dammit?*'

'Around that corner, I think. Why?'

Reed took off even before Ed stopped talking. He turned the corner, found himself in a darkened corridor — part of the hospital that had been closed down.

'Dammit, let's get some light down here!'

Spader spotted the switches and hit them. Fluorescents flickered overhead and slowly light twitched on all along the corridor.

At the far end Reed spotted a discarded trolley with a blanket on it.

The others crowded up behind him. 'Lilith's taken her,' Reed said for the benefit of Spader and Koenig. 'Down there.'

24

As Reed set off with Diana beside him, Spader grabbed his .38 from its holster. 'Give me your honest opinion, Rabbi,' he said. 'Is it *really* possible we could be dealing with a ten-thousand-year-old demon here?'

Koenig looked bleak. 'I wouldn't want to be the one who said it wasn't.'

As they went after Reed and Diana, the rabbi said: 'Not to sound negative or anything, but what's your plan if we *do* find them, Major?'

Reed glanced back at him. 'You mean your book doesn't have any magic spells to banish demons?'

'Sorry. I'm not Harry Potter.'

'Now you tell me.'

The gloomy corridor ended at a fire-door marked *TO ROOF*.

Unhesitatingly Reed pushed it open and stepped out onto the chilly, wind-whipped roof. It was a vast expanse dappled with patches of light snow, studded here and there with air conditioning units and a now-disused helipad that had been built back in the days when emergency cases were flown to Frankport as a matter of course.

Reed looked around, so frantic now that he missed them on his first urgent sweep. Then he caught a movement at the edge of the roof off to his right — a young blonde girl with her back to him and one foot resting against the low coping that surrounded it; a young blonde girl wearing a black vinyl raincoat and impractical red stiletto-heeled pumps who had called herself Lilith Adams and slept with him and then used him to pass on a devil-cursed computer to spread her own particular brand of sickness through a town that was already dying.

'*Lilith!*' he yelled.

She turned, Skylar in her grasp and all of Frankport sprawled out below her. She smiled at him. He saw Skylar's eyes widen, frightened more for Reed than for her own precarious position.

Reed moved slowly across the roof.

'Skylar,' he called. 'Scout. It's me, Reed. Can you hear me?'

'You're too late, hero,' Lilith said mockingly. 'Your little honey's already mine.'

'Only till I take her back.'

She feigned surprise. 'Well what do you know,' she hissed. 'You're *sober*.'

'Not too late to remedy that,' he said, edging closer. 'You, me, in bed with a bottle of VO.'

'You're hot in bed, I admit. But right now I've got more pressing things to do. And you're not going to stop me, Reed Devlin. No one is. You might think you know what I am. Maybe you *do*. But you can't even *begin* to imagine the power I possess.'

'And you can't even begin to imagine the power *Skylar* possesses,' he said. 'You picked the wrong kid this time, didn't you, Lilith? You finally picked on the one kid who has the power to stop you.'

'Not for long, hero.'

Lilith turned away from him and beneath her raincoat her muscles flexed as she prepared to throw Skylar off the

231

roof. But even as she did so Reed heard Spader, behind him, yell: '*Devlin! Get down!*'

He dropped flat just as Spader fired his .38. The bullet whacked Lilith in the right shoulder and punched her sideways, away from Skylar. Skylar swayed forward, close to passing out. Reed jumped up and yelled her name: '*Skylar! Scout! It's me, Reed!*'

She blinked, turned, saw him without really seeing him at all.

'*Come to me, baby!*' he yelled.

She moved just as Lilith, recovering from the impact of the bullet, tried to grab her. Somehow she had the presence of mind to dodge the demon's grasp and stumble-run toward Reed. Reed urged her on, arms outstretched, keeping his eyes on Lilith as she raised her hands as if trying to draw Skylar back with invisible reins.

'*Run!*' Reed yelled to Skylar.

Behind him Diana's voice joined in, desperate: '*Come on, kitten! Come to me!*'

Skylar ran past Reed with Lilith right behind her.

Without thinking Reed stepped into the demon's path.

Not giving her a chance to react he threw himself at her, and just before they clashed he saw something in her eyes that set his blood surging — surprise, and a glimmer of fear.

Then he hit her with every ounce of strength he possessed and drove her hard up against one of the air conditioning units. She slammed against it — the thin material bent and boomed, and before she could recover he punched her again, the blow snapping her head sideways.

But when she turned her face back to him she was grinning.

Not only that — her skin was now a heaving, seething mass of constantly-flexing green and black scales.

She grabbed him, effortlessly lifting him off his feet, and threw him aside. He flew through the air and then crashed onto the snowy roof.

Stunned, he tried to collect himself. As far as he could tell he hadn't broken anything. He rolled over and was about to get up when, suddenly, Lilith was right beside him. He looked up at her, at her hideously ugly face, and saw she was still grinning.

'Nice knowing you, Reed,' she said.

She raised her foot and slammed it down on his back.

The stiletto heel jammed deep into the meat below his left shoulder-blade. He cried out in pain and collapsed again.

For an interminable moment there was nothing but the searing fire of the wound, made a thousand times worse when Lilith ripped her heel out of his back. He flopped like a landed fish, fingers scraping at the thin layer of snow.

'*Mr. Devlin!*'

Skylar's voice cut through his agony, bringing him back to the present. At the same time he heard Lilith laughing in anticipation of tearing the life out of the one thing that could stop her — Skylar.

No way.

No fuckin' way.

Gritting his teeth, he forced himself to forget the pain and struggled to his knees. Lilith was staring at Skylar and the others, who were clustered in the doorway. Now, noticing him move, she looked disdain-fully at him.

'What, you want some more?' she began.

Reed jack-knifed his body, his legs sweeping hers right out from under her. Lilith landed hard on the roof with a roar of fury. Reed immediately got up and hurled himself at her. They both went sprawling.

She writhed under him like a snake, spitting, cursing, trying to rake him with her long nails. But he managed to straddle her, somehow caught her wrists and glared at her with equal fury and contempt.

'Sorry, baby,' he said. 'I know you normally like to be on top.'

Releasing one of her hands, he punched her full in her ugly, scaly face. He felt her nose break, her lips split, saw starlight glistening on the blood that spurted out, heard her scream with pain and rage.

He went to hit her again. But with a demonic howl, she threw him off. He flew several feet and again landed hard on the roof, the impact knocking the wind out of him.

It took everything he had, but he managed to get up. He stood there, swaying, dazed but knowing he mustn't pass out.

Lilith, now on her feet, glared at him, her face a mask of blood.

And she was *still* grinning.

'You don't get it, do you, Reed?' she said through pulpy lips. 'You're never going to beat me. *Never.*'

Before he could reply, she turned her back on him, walked sensuously to the edge of the roof and raised her arms high above her head.

Reed swayed and would have fallen had Rabbi Koenig not suddenly appeared at his side and grabbed him.

'What's she doing?' Reed gasped.

The rabbi shook his head, too shocked to speak.

Around them the night grew still and silent, as if the world had stopped turning and everything, everyone had been frozen in time.

'Dammit, what's she *doing?*'

She was *singing*.

Soft, low, a keening rise and fall of sound, the notes alien and unlike anything they had ever heard before. Discordant, jarring, no note seeming to match the one that came before it or the one that came in its wake . . .

. . . while at the edge of town the darkness seemed to . . . move.

25

Reed felt his sweat-pebbled skin tingle. It wasn't his imagination . . . *was* it? The darkness *was* moving, somehow; undulating, pushing forward and breaking up, breaking into . . .

'What the fuck *are* they?' he asked. '*Children?*'

That's what they looked like as they came surging down the street toward the hospital. Children ranging in age from eight to fourteen, all blonde, all violet-eyed, all possessing Lilith's human face.

'Not children,' Rabbi Koenig said, voice almost a sob. 'They are the *Lilin. Lilith's* children.'

Reed shook his head, close to tears himself. 'But she's supposed to *kill* her children. Every day she kills them. You *said* so.'

'I said that is what she was commanded by the Lord to do,' said Koenig. 'But Lilith has defied God before. What makes you think she wouldn't defy him *again?*'

Reed shook his head, remembering the things he'd seen scurrying across the benches at the high school playing field the night of the storm, the things he thought he'd seen racing past the stained glass windows at St. Mark's, backlit by the lightning. He thought of the thing that had crossed his path and vanished into an alley, which he'd dismissed as a stray dog, and the sound something had made running across the trailer roof while he and Lilith had been kissing.

He spun around and yelled: '*Spader!* Tell security they've got to lock all the doors right now!' And then he charged forward, determined to do what he should have done even before Lilith starting singing her weird —

Oh Christ.

It was a *lullaby.*

She was singing a *lullaby* to summon her children.

He lunged at her, intending to push her off the roof. But she heard or sensed him coming, stopped singing and twisted, her right hand blurred out and her fingers clutched his throat.

'Too late,' she said, her tongue long and snake-like, its end forked like that of a lizard. '*I* win.'

She pulled him close, so strong that he had no choice but to go with her. She wrenched him to the edge of the roof and made him look down even as the *lilin* — a hundred, two hundred, five hundred, maybe even thousand — reached the hospital and started to scurry up the walls toward the roof.

Reed instinctively tried to deny the evidence of his eyes. This wasn't happening, it *couldn't* be! The *lilin* were finding hand- and toe-holds between bricks and ledges and climbing fast and easily toward them, some already so close that he could see the baleful glare in their uncanny violet eyes.

There was another blur of movement and Lilith fell sideways. Reed staggered away from her, realizing dimly that Spader had used the distraction to sneak up and pistol-whip her.

'What's going on?' he demanded.

'We've got to get out of here,' Reed

said. 'We've got to keep Skylar safe.'

The first of the *lilin* hopped over the lip of the roof. It was a boy, maybe twelve, naked and scaly, the scales — incredibly fine — bristling and undulating as if propelled by some dark excitement.

'*Shoot it!*' yelled Reed.

Spader stood frozen, fascinated and repelled at the same time.

The *lilin* child opened its mouth and hissed at him. Its teeth were small and pointed.

A few days earlier it had introduced itself to Cameron Carlyle as Junior.

Reed snatched the gun from Spader's hand and fired. There was a red explosion where the boy's head had been.

'*Now, run!*' he shouted.

Sickened, Spader grabbed his gun back, hesitated, and then ran toward the rooftop door leading back into the hospital.

Even as Lilith climbed groggily to her feet, the rest of the *lilin* began to swarm over the lip of the roof like a colony of bizarre albino spiders.

Reed stared at them, momentarily

hypnotized. Then he shoved Rabbi Koenig and Lieutenant Spader ahead of him toward the door. 'Hurry!' Turning, he waited for Diana, with Skylar in her arms, to join him and then escorted them to the door.

When everyone was inside, Reed slammed the door shut and slid the bar into place to hold it shut. He felt Diana's eyes on him, wide, uncomprehending. He said, 'Don't ask,' and took Skylar from her.

'Go, go, go!' he told the others.

They all started down the first flight of stone steps. As they reached the bottom and paused there a moment, there was a violent thud above them.

They looked. Something slammed against the door from the outside. It made a small, fist-sized impression in the steel.

Spader blanched. 'Jesus . . . '

They backed up as the door started to shudder and more fist-prints made the steel bulge inward.

'That's not gonna hold for long,' Diana said.

Reed nodded in agreement. 'We've got to get Skylar out of here, now!'

'But — '

'She's the only thing that stands between Lilith and the rest of the world,' he said. 'Don't ask me why or how, but the other day I told Father Benedict he had a pipeline to God. I was wrong — it's *Skylar* who's got the pipeline. We lose her and we lose the only protection we have against Lilith.'

'But where can we go?'

The top hinge on the steel door was suddenly forced away from the frame.

'Anywhere that's not here,' Reed said. He and the others raced on down the next flight of steps. Spader jerked the door open, waited for the rabbi, Diana and Skylar to pass through then he and Reed followed. As one, they hurried along the corridor that led past the patients' rooms.

'*Everyone!*' yelled Spader, pushing out ahead. 'Stay in your rooms and keep the doors shut. You should be okay. Whatever comes down this hallway after us is only interested in us, so keep out of its way! If you can, call security and the Frankport PD. Tell them hell's breaking loose down here, the hospital's under siege and we need a SWAT team, pronto!'

Behind them the roof-door exploded inward and crashed to the floor. Diana looked over one shoulder and saw the doorway filled with — *kids?* — all naked, all blonde, all with the same peculiar violet eyes, all trying to be the first one inside, the first one to catch their prey and win their mother's approval.

Oh God.

Reed swept past Ed and Lorena. Ed said: 'What the hell's — ?'

'Get off this corridor!' Reed called back. 'Fort up in one of these rooms and don't open the door for anyone!'

He reached the elevators at the end of the corridor and punched the button. 'Come on . . . come on . . . '

The *lilin* poured through the door and sprinted toward them, an unstoppable flood.

'Shoot them!' Reed yelled at Spader.

The detective grudgingly raised his .38 and fired. Two of the lead *lilin* stumbled and fell, the ones immediately behind them tripping over the corpses.

The elevator doors slid open. Reed heard his own voice, high, scared. '*Inside! Quickly!*' And to Diana: '*Ground Floor!*'

Diana stabbed the button and the doors whispered shut. There was another thump from outside, another inward bulge of the elevator door and then they were descending.

Reed examined Skylar, who was barely conscious.

'What's the plan, Major?' Spader asked breathlessly.

'Wish I had one,' Reed said. 'If we can get Skylar to my pickup and out-run them . . . well, maybe the SWAT team can thin 'em out. I don't know. All I know is we have to keep Skylar aliv— '

The elevator ground to a shuddering halt.

Something landed on the roof, then another and another. Whoever was up there started pounding at the metal, leaving knuckle-prints with every blow.

'Everyone,' Spader said, 'cover your ears.' He aimed his .38 at the ceiling and fired another shot. On the other side some-thing screamed, there was a scrabbling sound, the sound of claws scratching steel, and then silence.

With a jolt the elevator continued on its way down.

'There must be a thousand of them,' fretted Rabbi Koenig. 'The parking lot is probably full of them.'

Reed said: 'Listen, all of you: I'll make a run for it, get the pickup and bring it back to the hospital doors. Be ready.'

Diana touched his arm. 'It's suicide, Reed.'

'Thanks for the encouragement.'

The elevator stopped and the doors opened onto the lobby. Security guards were milling around, not sure what they should be doing. At least they'd locked all the doors and windows.

One of the guards immediately tried to cut them off. 'Hey, you can't go out there. I don't know what those goddamn things are but they — '

Spader flashed his badge. 'Is this place secured?'

'As best as we could do it, yeah. Those

things . . . what the hell are they?'

'Killers,' Spader replied flatly. 'Now, I want you guys to watch the stairs and elevators, because they're already in the building and they're coming this way. Minute you see 'em, *shoot* 'em.'

The guard's eyes saucered. 'I can't do that. They're just kids.'

'You'll kill *them* or they'll kill *you*,' Spader said, reloading his weapon. Then: 'Here, Reed. Take my piece. I'll go for your pickup.'

'Forget it.'

'Makes more sense,' said Spader. 'I got two good legs.'

'And it was me who started this whole nightmare by giving that computer to Skylar in the first place. *I'll go!*'

'Then make it quick. We don't have much time.'

Reed glanced around, spotted a disused IV pole in the corner and went over to it. The pole had four hooks at the top end, where intravenous drips could be suspended. The bottom part was held in a splayed set of four casters by means of a retaining screw.

'Got a nail file?' he asked Diana.

She nodded and dug one out her bag. 'Here.'

He quickly loosened the retaining screw and held the pole like a spear.

'All right,' he said. 'I'll go through the revolving door. Soon as I'm through, lock it again, got that?'

Pale-faced, the security guard nodded.

There was a *ping* of sound as another elevator reached the ground floor. They all watched, hardly daring to breathe. A moment later the doors slid open.

Lilin poured into the lobby.

'*Go!*' yelled Spader, and emptied his gun into the demon children.

The guard unlocked the revolving door. Reed pushed against the glass and started it moving. Outside the other *lilin* were all pressed close to the toughened glass doors, pounding and scratching at them in their eagerness to kill.

Reed sucked in a breath —

The door opened out into the lot. He swung the pole at them, crushing one's face, one of the hooks gouging another one's eye out of its socket.

Clawed hands reached for him. He bent low and barreled through the mob of scaly, violet-eyed children, swinging the pole back and forth in front of him to clear a path.

Some of the *lilin* went after him. Others stayed where they were, continuing to hammer at the front doors.

The noise was tremendous. The *lilin* were howling and screeching as he knocked them aside. He felt them tugging at his jacket, his pants. One scratched his face. He whirled around and without meaning to skewered it through the middle. That made them howl even louder.

He shook the pole and the dead *lilin* fell off it.

But he was never going to reach the pickup. He saw that now.

There were just too many of them.

26

Whirling around, he prepared to do the only thing he could do in the circumstances — fight.

Taken by surprise they backed off for a second. Then one, who looked older than the rest, opened his mouth and made the weird, now-familiar trilling sound. At once the other *lilin* surged forward.

Before they could reach Reed, they were suddenly caught in a beam of light. They stopped as if bewildered. Moments later Officer Kelsey's patrol car slammed through them, throwing bodies everywhere. He stamped on the brake, thrust his pale face out the window and yelled: 'Jesus Christ, Major — what's goin' on here?'

Reed waved him on. '*Keep your windows closed and get out of here!*'

But Kelsey's appearance had bought him the time he needed to reach the pickup. He hurled the pole at the remaining *lilin*, forcing them back, and dived into the truck. Hitting the door locks, he started the engine. The truck growled to life, the headlights flared, and Reed got his first good look at the hospital.

The front of it was almost completely covered by *lilin*, some still swarming toward the roof, others hanging one-handed from the brickwork, looking back over their shoulders like children pretending to be monkeys, watching the drama unfolding in the parking lot.

God Almighty . . .

Reed floored the gas pedal. The truck leapt forward, smashing into the *lilin* that tried to block his path and hurling them aside. As the truck lurched over their bodies others jumped onto the hood, faces squashed up against the windshield.

Reed braked hard so he could dislodge the bodies and clear the view ahead. Several *lilin* fell off. He then punched the gas again and aimed the truck at the *lilin* clustered around the hospital entrance.

At the last moment he braked hard and the truck turned a sickening one-eighty. It smashed sideways-on into the knot of howling demon-kids, scattering them like bowling pins.

Inside the hospital Spader yelled, '*Now!*' and the guard unlocked the revolving door. Spader went first, wielding his reloaded .38. He shot one *lilin* through the forehead, another in the chest, a third in the face. Then he was at the side of the truck, tearing the passenger-side door open, herding Diana inside, passing Skylar to her, pushing Rabbi Koenig into the back seat and following —

One of the *lilin* grabbed him by the sleeve. He turned and shot it through the head, then threw himself into the truck and pulled the door shut behind him. *Lilin* fingers caught between the door and the frame, dragging the demon child along. Spader quickly opened the door, releasing the child's hand, and then slammed it shut again.

'*Drive, Devlin!*'

Reed jammed the truck into gear and sent it howling forward. Again the *lilin* hurled themselves at the fast-moving vehicle.

Some managed to cling to it; others fell and were crushed beneath its tires. The truck bumped and rocked as if it were riding over rough terrain, squelching *lilin* bodies as it went.

But more and more *lilin* were now leaping from the hospital walls to join the others in stopping the truck from escaping. They ran alongside it, howling and trilling and slapping at the windows. One window shattered, glass cascading over Rabbi Koenig.

'*Go, Reed! Go!*'

'*I'm trying to, goddammit!*'

More *lilin* leapt onto the roof, dropped to their knees and hammered at the metal. Others jumped into the bed and began attacking the rear window of the cab. Older *lilin* sprang onto the hood, punching or kicking at the windshield. Slowly but surely they covered the windows, blocking Reed's view of the lot. Their howling and hammering was so loud, he found it hard to concentrate.

He floored the gas pedal, desperately trying to get the truck to go faster. But the ever-increasing number of the *lilin* hanging all over it compressed the shock-absorbers, causing the truck to lurch from side to side and lose speed.

Amid all this chaos and bedlam, Skylar suddenly regained consciousness in Diana's arms. Seeing all the *lilin* faces leering at her, she grew alarmed.

'It's okay, kitten,' Diana soothed. 'It's okay . . . '

But of course it wasn't okay; and even in her feverish state Skylar seemed to know it. She struggled to escape Diana's grip, at the same time pointing with her hand at the *lilin* plastered over the windshield. Diana hugged her closer and tried to soothe her.

'I know, honey, but we'll lose them any minute now . . . '

Skylar shook her head urgently, her eyes wide, her mouth parted, little mewling sounds coming from her. She hit the windshield with her forefinger. Outside, the *lilin* tried to snatch at it. Then she moved her hand in a sort of wavy gesture. Amazingly, Reed heard the squeak it made running down the glass.

'What's she trying to do?' yelled Spader.

'I dunno. Write something?'

'Yeah, yeah, looks like,' Reed said. He watched as Skylar traced a letter on the glass. 'That's an *S*, isn't it?'

'Yes,' Diana said. Then: 'Her name! She's trying to write her name.'

Her voice seemed to spur Skylar on. Again she ran her forefinger down the windshield, describing another *S* shape.

'No, no, I'm wrong,' Diana said. 'I think she's delirious.'

A third time Skylar did it.

And then . . .

She collapsed back into Diana's arms, as if exhausted . . . or dying.

Reed felt his whole world — what was left of it — tilt drunkenly. 'Skylar?' he said. And then, more urgently: 'Skylar, honey — ?'

'It's all right, Reed. She just passed out agai— '

He wasn't listening. Something else had claimed his attention. At first he thought it was just his imagination, but no . . . the *lilin* really *were* starting to ease off in their attack. They stopped hammering at the truck and in ones and twos slid off the hood, while others jumped out of the bed or off the roof. Gradually the weight of their bodies lessened. The truck stopped lurching from side to side and Reed felt it rise off its overburdened springs.

'Brace yourselves,' he told the others. 'We're getting out of here.'

Diana stopped him. 'Wait, Reed. What's happening out there?'

'I don't know, and right now I don't give a rat's ass. Could be they're just getting their second wind — '

'No,' said Rabbi Koenig, leaning forward and pointing. 'No. *Look!*'

He pointed toward the night sky — to a spot in the middle-distance about forty degrees off the horizon, where three stars twinkled in a roughly triangular formation.

The *lilin* were staring at them as well.

Reed looked around. The parking lot was jammed with *lilin*, all of them now facing the eastern sky, all seemingly entranced by the three stars.

The three stars that were slowly growing larger.

27

'Now what?' asked Spader.

A sob of hope escaped the rabbi. 'I think I know,' he whispered. 'Oh Lord, I think I know.'

'Well, share the wealth, will you?'

'Skylar,' Koenig said. 'She's summoned them.'

'Summoned . . . ?'

'Snvi, Snsvi and Smnglof,' he said.

'*Gesundheit*,' said Reed. 'Now say that in English.'

'In English they are known as Senoy, Sansenoy and Semangelof,' the rabbi said. 'They're the angels God sent after Lilith when she first left Adam. Had she returned to become Adam's mate, God would have forgiven her. But she refused to return, claiming that she had only been created to cause sickness and death to infants. However, she swore to the three angels that whenever she saw their names or forms, she would allow the infants

257

under their protection to live.'

'And now they're here to kick ass?'

'Earthy,' said Rabbi Koenig, 'but accurate, I think.'

By this time the lights had descended to the far end of Main Street. Almost too bright to look at, Reed was nevertheless sure he could make out a figure within each radiant aura. Each one seemed to be wrapped in some sort of diaphanous garb that fell from one shoulder. Each had hair that was long and silver. Their eyes were deep and dark, their skin milk-pale, their bodies small and toned. And from the backs of each there seemed to project two long, charcoal-gray wings, slim and finely feathered.

A white dove sat on each right wrist.

'It's true,' Rabbi Koenig said as they finally settled to earth. 'It's all true. It was *always* true.'

A familiar, high trilling sound suddenly cut through the air and made them all wince. A ripple seemed to pass through the assembled *lilin*. Slowly they began to shuffle forward, as if forming a line of battle.

Taking a chance, Reed unlocked his door and got out. Diana called his name.

He ignored her . . . and the *lilin* ignored him. Their entire attention was now focused on the three glowing figures at the far end of Main Street; he, Skylar and the others were — at least temporarily — forgotten.

Again the curious trilling carried across Frankport. Reed looked up and saw Lilith standing on the edge of the roof, naked now, arms outstretched, eyes ranging across her children . . . her army.

And then —

As one the thousand or more children began to trill some kind of war-cry of their own, and as if at some silent command charged toward the three angels.

Reed quickly climbed into the bed of the pickup in order to get a better view. The others chanced it and left the truck so they could do likewise.

The *lilin* swarmed toward their enemies, running on two feet or all fours, bounding and leaping, some jumping over parked cars, others racing diagonally up and across the walls of buildings, and the sound they made as they joined battle chilled Reed's blood.

The angels, Senoy, Sansenoy and Semangelof, watched them come, watched as the horde of demon children surged back up the street in a monstrous flood.

Then Senoy stepped forward and something white flared from her eyes. It resembled a laser beam but was much thicker. The light, white at its center and yellow at its outer edges, swept from side to side — torching everything it touched.

The light seemed to build and build until suddenly there was a great explosion.

Body parts flew through the air as the first wave of *lilin* were vaporized. Some of those following managed to avoid the beams of light. But there was no escape. At once the center angel, Sansenoy, stared fixedly at them . . . the piercing light from her eyes also blasting the demon children to pieces.

Semangelof concentrated on the *lilin* who were scuttling across the walls of the buildings on both sides of Main Street. Working swiftly, she picked them off one by one, and with every flare and crash of sound and sudden crumbling of masonry, another of Lilith's children died.

Perched on the edge of the hospital roof Lilith watched in fury as the angels began to stride forward to meet her minions. Horrified, she saw her blonde, violet-eyed children cut down in great swathes. Soon Main Street was littered with charred bodies and still-smoking chunks of flesh. Slowly the trilling faded. The explosions of light connecting with demonic flesh grew fewer and farther between. Gradually . . . gradually . . . the battle closed on its inevitable outcome.

Lilith screeched, enraged. Looking up, Reed saw her bend at the knees, saw her claw-like fingers flex and curl with the wrath that was building inside her. Then, with a jolt, he realized that she was looking down at him and her violet eyes were aflame with a hatred that could never be quenched.

She launched herself off the hospital roof and as she did so she underwent a lightning transformation. She shrank in on herself, her scaly flesh appeared to mottle, and then, with startling suddenness, it was complete; she was no longer a woman, nor a demon masquerading as one — she was a screech owl.

And she was diving straight at —

Realizing what she was going to do Reed turned to his companions and yelled: '*Skylar!* Somebody get her back in the truck!'

While Rabbi Koenig did just that, Lieutenant Spader took aim and emptied his .38 at the diving bird.

Not one bullet found its mark.

Faster she dove, dropping with eyes ablaze and talons ready —

Then there came more fluttering of wings. Diana looked over her shoulder in time to see the three angels raise their right arms and the doves that were perched there suddenly take to the night sky.

As one they homed in on the diving owl . . . and as one they smashed into it, battering it away from its intended course. Then, without mercy, they attacked it.

A short, vicious struggle ensued as the owl sought to defend itself against its three enemies. Birds shrieked, feathers were torn loose and drifted to earth . . . But though the screech owl desperately fought to defend itself, inexorably its struggles weakened until it, too, fell from the sky and crashed to earth.

At last silence reined over Frankport.

The doves flew back to their mistresses and settled obediently upon their outstretched wrists. Then the angels left the ground and seemed to glide to the hospital parking lot, until they were hovering directly over Reed's pickup.

A gentle, faintly bluish light shone down on Reed and Diana, on Spader, and Koenig . . . and Skylar. And as Reed watched, the lesions on Skylar's face began to shrink and fade.

It took only moments. Then were gone and there was not even the faintest mark left on her skin to show that they had ever been there.

Satisfied, the angels turned their faces toward the hospital, focusing themselves on the fifth floor . . . and the Isolation Ward.

Reed watched, conscious now of nothing save the angels and what they were doing to undo the damage Lilith had wrought. Beside him, Rabbi Koenig wept softly.

Then there came a great, unexpected

burst of pure white light, a strange sense of everything somehow moving backward and somehow *undoing* itself, and then —

It was over.

The angels were gone.

The bodies of the *lilin* were gone.

And the screech owl was gone.

28

For a while they struggled to get their heads around everything they'd just seen. It was practically impossible. Then Reed grew dimly aware of staff and patients gradually appearing at the hospital windows, of the security guards unlocking the building and coming outside. They stood there and stared, open-mouthed, at the now-empty night sky, listening to the sound of first-responder sirens in the distance, slowly growing louder.

'*Baby!*'

Lorena Lewis' voice cut through the night. She and Ed ran across the lot toward them, and Skylar, finding the strength to grin now, went to meet them.

Diana leaned back against the pickup and closed her eyes. 'Shit,' she said.

Trying unsuccessfully to inspect his wounded shoulder, Reed limped over to her. 'You okay?'

'Next question.'

'What's wrong?'

'Don't you get it?' She gestured about her, too exasperated to speak for a moment. Then: 'I just had a front-row seat for the biggest story in the history of the world and I've got nothing to back it up with.'

'What do you mean?'

'No pictures. No video. Not even a soundtrack! Zilch! *Now* do you get it?'

Reed nodded.

'Zilch!' she repeated. 'Not-one-goddamn-thing! Nothing to prove that it ever happened. Just a bunch of eyewitnesses who'll probably never agree on exactly what they saw — '

'*Diana!*'

She turned as Gary Chalmers appeared from behind some nearby parked cars.

'*Gary?*'

He came jogging up. 'Jumping Judas! Did you just *see* that?'

'*See* it?' Diana said. 'For chrissake, I was *part* of it, you dork! We all were! Where the hell did you spring from, anyway?'

'Around,' he said vaguely.

'Dammit, Gary, I'm in no mood to play fucking games — '

'Okay, okay . . . Earlier tonight, I . . . I heard you talking to a guy in your hotel room.'

'That was me,' Reed said.

'I know,' Gary said. 'Then you two took off and . . . I, uhm . . . well, I was only trying to look out for you, Di.'

'You mean you *followed* me?'

'Uh-huh — to the Lewis' place. I didn't want to butt in when you got there — looked like they already had enough problems. So I started to call your cell, but then that cop and the rabbi showed up and . . . well, long story short, I followed you here and — '

'Wait a minute,' she said as it dawned on her. 'If you were here then . . . that means you saw what happened, right?'

'Yup.'

She studied him, almost afraid to ask. 'Tell me you brought your camera.'

'Camera?'

'Aw, shit!' she said. ''Mean you *didn't?*'

'I mean,' he said, holding up his portable digital camera, 'it's just like my

267

Amex card. I never leave home without it.'

Diana gaped, her expression a mixture of joy and relief. 'Are you telling me you actually *got* it?'

'Yup.'

'You got everything that just happened? *Everything*?'

'Yeah, yeah.' He grinned. 'Everything! All exclusive!'

'Oh-you-crazy-nerdy-wonderful-bastard!' Giggling like a schoolgirl, she wrapped her arms around him. 'Well, lemme see it, for God's sake!' she said. 'Let me see it!'

'Okay, okay, don't get your panties in a wedge.' Gary pressed the replay button on his camera and handed it to her. 'Here. Enjoy.'

The three of them stared into the view-finder, but saw nothing. Gary reached over and pressed the replay button again. But the little screen remained stubbornly blank.

They all looked at each other, puzzled.

'I don't believe this,' said Gary. 'It was working fine before.'

'*Well, it ain't working now*,' Diana said. 'And that's all that counts.'

Gary watched her, waiting for the inevitable explosion. But to his surprise she only released a long, resigned sigh. 'Ah, what the hell,' she said. 'I guess God's camera-shy.'

She saw the way Gary was looking at her, and with a new understanding of herself said: 'It's not the end of the world. I mean, we've still got a job, such as it is, and in today's economy we should just be grateful for that.'

Reed started to agree with her — then stopped as Diana's cell buzzed.

She dug it out and answered it. 'Yeah? . . . Yes, this is she . . . ' She looked at Reed and Gary and shrugged, indicating she didn't know the caller. 'No, you didn't wake me up. Go ahead . . . ' She listened, her expression growing more inscrutable as the caller continued. 'Y-Yes,' she said finally, her eyebrows arching, 'Yes, of course, I understand . . . 'Bye.'

She ended the call and stared at her cell.

'Who was that?' Reed asked.

Diana looked at Gary and slowly shook her head. 'We've just been bought out,' she said, still in shock. 'The station — WDWC-TV — we got new owners.'

Gary's shoulders slumped. 'Oh shit, don't tell me. We've all been fired.'

'Not all of us.' She suddenly beamed. 'But *Jamie* has.'

'Jamie?' Gary echoed.

'Jamie-college-fucking-graduate-him-self.'

Gary punched the air. '*Yessss!*'

'There's more,' Diana said, sounding as if she didn't believe it. 'The new program manager wants to talk to me about going back to anchoring the six o'clock news!'

29

It was one of those crisp, wintry-bright, Michigan days. Reed opened the door of his trailer, stepped out and stretched as if he hadn't a care in the world.

★ ★ ★

Immediately the crowd of reporters who had gathered on the other side of the police tape that now cordoned off Reed's property started calling to him.

'Major Devlin! How about that exclusive interview?'

'Yeah, yeah, you can name your own price!'

'Over here, Major! Smile for the camera!'

Reed ignored them all. Over the last two weeks he'd had plenty of practice. Frankport had been inundated by out-of-towners, all eager to talk to anyone who'd witnessed the events of that fateful night.

271

He went directly to his pickup and climbed inside. He eased the truck toward the police tape and nodded his thanks when Officer Kelsey pulled it up so that he could drive underneath it.

As soon as he turned the first corner and could no longer be seen by the crowd, he said: 'All right, scout. You can come out now.'

The old blanket on the jump-seat stirred and Skylar sat up.

'How did you know I was there?' she asked.

''Cause I knew you'd want to be with me on my big day.' He looked at her in the rear-view mirror. 'How long you been waiting, anyway?'

She grinned. 'Since long before your fans arrived.'

She noticed that he'd shaved, was wearing a clean white shirt over his new blue jeans, and most importantly that he was sober. 'You clean up real pretty, Mr. Devlin.'

'Reed.

'Mr. Devlin.'

Main Street was already busy. Skylar

quickly ducked out of sight again as they passed some tourists — what Frankport was already calling pilgrims. When she sat up a few seconds later she frowned. 'Hey, this isn't the way to the town hall.'

'I gotta make a stop first.'

'Where?'

'Bill's Liquor Store.' Off her look of shock he said: 'There's no way I can face my first AA meeting without a drink.'

Skylar was silent for a moment, then laughed. 'That was a joke, right?'

'You're learning.'

At the end of Main he turned into the parking lot outside RadioShack. Here, Diana was waiting for them beside her Camry, a large RadioShack bag in hand.

'What's going on?' asked Skylar.

He ignored her and got out. Determined to get an answer, she followed him. They went over to Diana, and Diana handed the bag to Skylar. 'Here you go, kitten.'

Puzzled, Skylar peered inside the bag. It contained a boxed, brand-new Deltium T-40 laptop. 'Oh, ma-a-an!' But her joy suddenly turned to suspicion. 'I'm not giving up my old laptop.'

'This isn't charity,' said Reed.

'Excuse me, I never said it was.' She looked at Diana. 'But I have to work it off.'

Diana looked quizzically at Reed, who said: 'It's a Skylar thing.'

Diana turned back to Skylar. 'How about a hug, then?'

Skylar happily obliged.

They climbed into the Camry and Diana drove them to the town hall, where weekly AA meetings were held.

Reed studied the building uneasily. 'I'd like to promise you both that this is the last of my boozing. But you can guess how many times I've screwed up in the past.'

'About the same number that I threatened to quit WDWC,' Diana replied. 'Stop worrying, Reed. You'll be fine. You won the Medal of Honor, for chrissake. This'll be a piece of cake.'

'Then why am I so freaking nervous?'

'Because this is the first day of the rest of your life,' said Skylar.

Diana leaned close and pecked Reed

on the cheek. 'Go on. Get your butt in there and strike a blow for temperance!'

He got out. So did Skylar. Taking his hand, she walked him to the steps that led up into the building. 'She's cool,' she said.

'Diana?' He shrugged. 'She's okay. For a news anchor, I mean.'

'She'd make an awesome wife.'

'Whoa, there, scout! I've only known her a couple of weeks.'

'If that don't bother her, it shouldn't bother you.'

'Thanks for the kind words.' He paused as they reached the steps. 'Look, I've been thinking. While I'm busy climbing on the wagon, why don't you go fix that Superman figure for me, okay?'

'You gonna yell at me again if I do?'

'I never yelled at you the first time . . . Oh, I might've raised my voice a little, but — ' Her look of reproach made him grin. 'Okay, so I yelled. Big deal.'

'It *is* a big deal. Anyway, what is it with you and that Superman figure?'

'I like Superman. Always have.'

'Yeah, but why? *Why* Superman?'

'Why is it so important for you to know?'

''Cause it's a secret, and we promised not to keep secrets, remember?'

He couldn't argue with that. 'I like him because . . . Dammit, my dad liked him, that's why.'

She cocked her at him. 'Your *dad*? Excuse me, but you didn't *like* your dad. Told me so, lots of times, 'specially when you were drunk.'

'I *didn't* like him,' Reed said. 'I blamed him for a medical condition that runs in my family, resented him for giving me what I thought was a death sentence. But that was wrong. He was as much a victim of it as I am — *might* be. Only by then it was too late, and he was already gone.'

Skylar sighed. 'Let me get this straight,' she said. 'You kept the Superman comic books because they belonged to your dad, but you won't glue on Superman's head 'cause you didn't like him?'

'Something like that.'

She studied him, clearly perplexed. Then she took a dollar from her change purse and slipped it into the envelope containing money for the starving children in Africa.

'Boy, Mr. Devlin,' she said, grinning. 'And you think *I'm* fucked up.'

THE END

We do hope that you have enjoyed reading this large print book.

Did you know that all of our titles are available for purchase?

We publish a wide range of high quality large print books including:
Romances, Mysteries, Classics
General Fiction
Non Fiction and Westerns

Special interest titles available in large print are:
The Little Oxford Dictionary
Music Book, Song Book
Hymn Book, Service Book

Also available from us courtesy of Oxford University Press:
Young Readers' Dictionary
(large print edition)
Young Readers' Thesaurus
(large print edition)

For further information or a free brochure, please contact us at:
Ulverscroft Large Print Books Ltd.,
The Green, Bradgate Road, Anstey,
Leicester, LE7 7FU, England.
Tel: (00 44) **0116 236 4325**
Fax: (00 44) **0116 234 0205**

Other titles in the
Linford Mystery Library:

NEW CASES FOR DOCTOR MORELLE

Ernest Dudley

Young heiress Cynthia Mason lives with her violent stepfather, Samuel Kimber, the controller of her fortune — until she marries. So when she becomes engaged to Peter Lorrimer, she fears Kimber's reaction. Peter, due to call and take her away, talks to Kimber in his study. Meanwhile, Cynthia has tiptoed downstairs and gone — she's vanished without trace. Her friend Miss Frayle, secretary to the criminologist Dr. Morelle, tries to find her — and finds herself a target for murder!

THE EVIL BELOW

Richard A. Lupoff

'*Investigator seeks secretary, amanuensis, and general assistant. Applicant must exhibit courage, strength, willingness to take risks and explore the unknown . . .* ' In 1905, John O'Leary had newly arrived in San Francisco. Looking for work, he had answered the advert, little understanding what was required for the post — he'd try anything once. In America he found a world of excitement and danger . . . and working for Abraham ben Zaccheus, San Francisco's most famous psychic detective, there was never a dull moment . . .

A STORM IN A TEACUP

Geraldine Ryan

In the first of four stories of mystery and intrigue, *A Storm in a Teacup*, Kerry has taken over the running of her aunt's café. After quitting her lousy job and equally lousy relationship with Craig, it seemed the perfect antidote. But her chef, with problems of his own, disrupts the smooth running of the café. Then, 'food inspectors' arrive, and vanish with the week's takings. But Kerry remembers something important about the voice of one of the bogus inspectors . . .

SÉANCE OF TERROR

Sydney J. Bounds

Chalmers decides to attend one of Dr. Lanson's nightly séances because it's somewhere warm to rest his weary feet. A decision he regrets when a luminous cloud forms above the assembled people. Strangely, from the cloud comes a warning: someone there is about to die to prevent them from revealing secrets. A man defiantly leaps to his feet, the lights are extinguished, the man's voice is cut off and an ear-piercing shriek reverberates around the room . . .